HARRIGAN

MAX BRAND

PHOENIX RIDER

an imprint of

MANOR

Rockville, Maryland

ISBN: 978-1-60450-400-2

www.PhoenixRider.com
Great Westerns at Great Prices

Published by Phoenix Rider
an imprint of Arc Manor
P. O. Box 10339
Rockville, MD 20849-0339
www.ArcManor.com

Printed in the United States of America / United Kingdom

Only $3.99

www.PhoenixRider.com

Incredible Westerns at Incredible Prices

Only $3.99

www.PhoenixRider.com

Incredible Westerns at Incredible Prices

All prices as of September 2008 and subject to change without notice

CHAPTER 1

"THAT FELLOW with the red hair," said the police captain as he pointed.

"I'll watch him," the sergeant answered.

The captain had raided two opium dens the day before, and the pride of accomplishment puffed his chest. He would have given advice to the sheriff of Oahu that evening.

He went on: "I can pick some men out of the crowd by the way they walk, and others by their eyes. That fellow has it written all over him."

The red-headed man came nearer through the crowd. Because of the warmth, he had stuffed his soft hat into a back pocket, and now the light from a window shone steadily on his hair and made a fire of it, a danger signal. He encountered the searching glances of the two officers and answered with cold, measuring eyes, like the gaze of a prize fighter who waits for a blow. The sergeant turned to his superior with a grunt.

"You're right," he nodded.

"Trail him," said the captain, "and take a man with you. If that fellow gets into trouble, you may need help."

He stepped into his automobile and the sergeant beckoned to a nearby policeman.

"Akana," he said, "we have a man-sized job tonight. Are you feeling fit?"

The Kanaka smiled without enthusiasm.

"The man of the red hair?"

The sergeant nodded, and Akana tightened his belt. He had eaten fish baked in ti leaves that evening.

He suggested: "Morley has little to do. His beat is quiet. Shall I tell him to come with us?"

"No," grinned the sergeant, and then looked up and watched the broad shoulders of the red-haired man, who advanced through the crowd as the prow of a ship lunges through the waves. "Go get Morley," he said abruptly.

But Harrigan went on his way without misgivings, not that he forgot the policeman, but he was accustomed to stand under the suspicious eye of the law. In all the course of his wanderings it had been upon him. His coming was to the men in uniform like the sound of the battle trumpet to the cavalry horse. This, however, was Harrigan's first night in Honolulu, and there was much to see, much to do. He had rambled through the streets; now he was headed for the

Ivilei district. Instinct brought him there, the still, small voice which had guided him from trouble to trouble all his life.

At a corner he stopped to watch a group of Kanakas who passed him, wreathed with leis and thrumming their ukuleles. They sang in their soft, many-voweled language and the sound was to Harrigan like the rush and lapse of water on a beach, infinitely soothing and as lazy as the atmosphere of Honolulu. All things are subdued in the strange city where East and West meet in the middle of the Pacific. The gayest crowds cannot quite disturb the brooding peace which is like the promise of sleep and rest at sunset. It was not pleasing to Harrigan. He frowned and drew a quick, impatient breath, muttering: "I'm not long for this joint. I gotta be moving."

He joined a crowd which eddied toward the center of Ivilei. In there it was better. Negro soldiers, marines from the *Maryland*, Kanakas, Chinamen, Japanese, Portuguese, Americans; a score of nationalities and complexions rubbed shoulders as they wandered aimlessly among the many bright-painted cottages.

Yet even in that careless throng of pleasure-seekers no one rubbed shoulders with Harrigan. The flame of his hair was like a red lamp which warned them away. Or perhaps it was his eye, which seemed to linger for a cold, incurious instant on every face that approached. He picked out the prettiest of the girls who sat at the windows chatting with all who passed. He did not have to shoulder to win a way through the crowd of her admirers.

She was a *hap haoli*, with the fine features of the Caucasian and the black of hair and eye which shows the islander. A rounded elbow rested on the sill of the window; her chin was cupped in her hand.

"Send these away," said Harrigan, and leaned an elbow beside hers.

"Oh," she murmured; then: "And if I send them away?"

"I'll reward you."

"Reward?"

For answer he dragged a crimson carnation from the buttonhole of a tall man who stood at his side.

"What in hell—" began the victim, but Harrigan smiled and the other drew slowly back through the crowd.

"Now send them away."

She looked at him an instant longer with a light coming slowly up behind her eyes. Then she leaned out and waved to the chuckling semicircle.

"Run away for a while," she said; "I want to talk to my brother."

She patted the thick red hair to emphasize the relationship, and the little crowd departed, laughing uproariously. Harrigan slipped the carnation into the jetty hair. His hand lingered a moment against the soft masses, and she drew it down, grown suddenly serious.

"There are three policemen in the shadow of that cottage over there. They're watching you."

"Ah-h!"

The sound was so soft that it was almost a sigh, but she shivered perceptibly.

"What have you been doing?"

He answered regretfully: "Nothing."

"They're coming this way. The man who had the carnation is with them. You better beat it."

"Nope. I like it here."

She shook her head, but the flame was blowing high now in her eyes. A hand fell on Harrigan's shoulder.

"Hey!" said the sergeant in a loud voice.

Harrigan turned slowly and the sergeant's hand fell away. The man of the carnation was far in the background.

"Well?"

"That flower. You can't get away with little tricks like that. You better be starting on. Move along."

Harrigan glanced slowly from face to face. The three policemen drew closer together as if for mutual protection.

"Please—honey!" urged the whisper of the girl.

The hand of Harrigan resting on the window sill had gathered to a hard-bunched fist, white at the knuckles, but he nodded across the open space between the cottages.

"If you're looking for work," he said, "seems as though you'd find a handful over there."

A clatter of sharp, quick voices rose from a group of Negro soldiers gathering around a white man. No one could tell the cause of the quarrel. It might have been anything from an oath to a blow.

"Watch him," said Harrigan. "He looks like a man." He added plaintively: "But looks are deceivin'."

The center of the disturbance appeared to be a man indeed. He was even taller than Harrigan and broader of shoulder, and, like the latter, there was a suggestion of strength in him which could not be defined by his size alone. At the distance they could guess his smile as he faced the clamoring mob.

"Break in there!" ordered the sergeant to his companions, and started toward the angry circle.

As he spoke, they heard one of the Negroes curse and the fist of the tall man darted at the face of a soldier and drove him toppling back among his comrades. They closed on the white man with a yell; a passing group of their compatriots joined the affray; the whole mass surged in around the tall fellow. Harrigan's head went back and his eyes half closed like a critic listening to an exquisite symphony.

"Ah-h!" he whispered to himself. "Watch him fight!"

The policemen struck the outer edge of the circle with drawn clubs, but there they stopped. They could not dent that compacted mass. The soldiers struggled manfully, but they were held at bay. Harrigan could see the heaving shoulders of the defender over the heads of the assailants, and the crack of hard-driven fists. The attackers were crushed together and had little room to swing their arms with full force, while the big man stood with his back against the wall of the cottage and made every smashing punch count.

As if by common assent, the soldiers suddenly desisted and gave back from this deadly fighter. His bellow of triumph rang over the clamor. His hat was off; his long black hair stood straight up in the wind; and he leaped after them with flailing arms.

But now the police had managed to pry their way into the mass by dint of indiscriminate battering. As the black-haired man came face to face with the sergeant, the light gleamed on a high-swung club that thudded home; and the big man dropped out of sight. He came up again almost at once, but with men draped from every portion of his body. The soldiers and police had joined forces, and once more a dozen men clutched him, spilling over him like football players in a scrimmage. He was knocked from his feet by the impact.

"Coming!" shouted Harrigan.

He raced with long strides, head lowered and back bowed until his long arms nearly swept the ground. Gathering impetus at every stride, he crushed into the floundering heap of arms and legs. The police sergeant rose and whirled with lifted club. Harrigan grunted with joy as he dug his left into the man's midsection. The sergeant collapsed upon the ground, embracing his stomach with both arms. Harrigan jerked away the upper layers of the attackers and dragged the black-haired man to his feet.

"Shoulder to shoulder!" thundered Harrigan, and smote Officer Akana upon the point of the chin.

The victory was not yet won. The black soldiers of Uncle Sam's regular army need not take second place to any body of troops in the world. These men had tasted their own blood and they came tearing in now for revenge.

Harrigan, standing full in front of the rescued man until the latter should have recovered his breath, found food for both fists, and his love of battle was fed. The other man had fought stiffly erect, standing with feet braced to give the weight of his whole body to every punch; Harrigan raged back and forth like a panther, avoiding blows by the catlike agility of his movements, which left both hands free to strike sledge-hammer blows. Presently he heard a chuckling at his side. Out of the corner of his eye he saw the black-haired man come into the battle, straight and stiff as before, with long arms shooting out like pistons.

It was a glorious sight. Something made Harrigan's heart big; rose and swelled his throat; rose again and came as a wild yell upon his tongue. The unfortunates who have faced Irish legions in battle know that yell. The soldiers did not know it, and they held back for a moment. Something else lowered their spirits still more. It was the clanging of the police patrol as it swung to a halt and a body of reserves poured out.

"Here comes our finish!" panted Harrigan to his comrade in arms. "But oh, man, I'm thinkin' it was swate while it lasted!"

In his great moments the Irish brogue thronged thick upon his tongue.

"Finish, hell!" grunted the other. "After me, lad!"

And lowering his head like a bull, he drove forward against the crowd. Harrigan caught the idea in a flash. He put his shoulder to the hip of his friend. They became a flying wedge with the jabbing fists of the black-haired man for a point—and they sank into the mass of soldiers like a hot knife into butter, shearing them apart.

There were few who wished more action, for the police reserves were capturing man after man. One or two resisted, but a revolver fired straight in the air put a sudden period to such thoughts. The crowd scattered in all directions and Harrigan was taking to his heels among the rest when an iron hand caught his shoulder and jerked him to a halt. It was the black-haired man.

"Easy," he cautioned. He pulled a cap out and settled it upon his head. Harrigan followed suit with his soft hat.

"Are you after givin' yourself away to the law?" he queried, bewildered.

"Steady, you fool," said the other; "they're only after the ones who run away."

An excited Kanaka confronted them with brandished club.

"What's the cause of the disturbance, officer?" asked the big man.

The policeman for answer waved them away and darted after a running soldier.

"I'll be damned!" murmured Harrigan, and his eyes dwelt on his companion's face almost tenderly.

They were at the edge of the crowd when a shrill voice called: "Those two big men! Halt 'em! Stand!"

Officer Akana ran through the crowd with his regulation Colt brandished above his head.

"The time's come!" said Harrigan's new friend, and broke into a run.

CHAPTER 2

THEY WERE past the thick of the mob now and they dodged rapidly among the cottages until the clamor of police fell away to a murmur behind them, and they swung out onto the narrow, dark street which led back toward the heart of Honolulu. For ten minutes they strode along without a word. Under the light of a street lamp they stopped of one accord.

"I'm McTee."

"I'm Harrigan."

The gripping of the hands was more than fellowship; it was like a test of strength which left each uncertain of the other's resources. They were exactly opposite types. McTee was long of face, with an arched, cruel nose, gleaming eyes, heavy, straight brows which pointed up and gave a touch of the Mephistophelian to his expression, a narrow, jutting chin, and lips habitually compressed to a thin line. It was a handsome face, in a way, but it showed such a brutal dominance that it inspired fear first and admiration afterward.

Such a man must command. He might be only the boss of a gang of laborers, or he might be a financier, but never in any case an underling. Altogether he combined physical and intellectual strength to such a degree that both men and women would have stopped to look at him, and once seen he would be remembered.

On the other hand, in Harrigan one felt only force, not directed and controlled as in McTee, but impulsive, irregular, irresponsible, uncompassed. He carried a contradiction in his face. The heavy, hard-cut jaw, the massive cheekbones, the stiff, straight upper lip indicated merely brutal endurance and energy, but these qualities were tempered by possibilities of tenderness about the lips and by the singular lights forever changing in the blue eyes. He would be hard for the shrewdest judge to understand, for the simple reason that he did not know himself.

In looking at McTee, one asked: "What is he?" In looking at Harrigan, the question was: "What will he become?"

"Stayin' in town long?" asked Harrigan, and his voice was a little wistful.

"I'm bound out tonight."

"So long, then."

"So long."

They turned on their heels into opposite streets without further words, with no thanks given for service rendered, with no exchange of congratulations for the danger they had just escaped. That parting proved them hardened knights of the road which leads across the world and never turns back home.

Harrigan strode on full of thought. His uncertain course brought him at last to the waterfront, and he idled along the black, odorous docks until he came to a pier where a ship was under steam, making ready to put out to sea. The spur touched the heart of Harrigan. The urge never failed to prick him when he heard the scream of a steamer's horn as it put to sea. It brought the thoughts of far lands and distant cities.

He strolled out to the pier and watched the last ropes cast loose. The ship was not large, and even in the dark it seemed dingy and dilapidated. He guessed that, big or small, this boat would carry her crew to some distant quarter of the world, and therefore to a place to be desired.

A strong voice gave an order from the deck—a hard voice with a ring in it like the striking of iron against iron. Harrigan glanced up with a start of recognition, and by the light of a swinging lantern he saw McTee. If he were in command, this ship was certainly going to a far port. Black water showed between the dock and the ship. In a moment more it would be beyond reach, and that thought decided Harrigan. He made a few paces back, noted the aperture in the rail of the ship where the gangplank was being drawn in, then ran at full speed and leaped high in the air.

The three sailors at the rail shouted their astonishment as Harrigan struck the edge of the gangplank, reeled, and then pitched forward to his knees. He rose and shook himself like a cat that has dropped from a high fence to the ground.

"What're you?"

"I'm the extra hand."

And Harrigan ran up the steps to the bridge. There he found McTee with the first and second mates.

"McTee," he said, "I came on your ship by chance an' saw you. If you *can* use an extra hand, let me stay. I'm footfree an' I need to be movin' on."

Even through the gloom he caught the glint of the Scotchman's eye.

"Get off the bridge!" thundered McTee.

"But I'm Harrigan, and—"

McTee turned to his first and second mates.

"Throw that man off the bridge!" he ordered.

Harrigan didn't wait. He retreated down the steps to the deck and went to the rail. A wide gap of swarthy water now extended between the ship and the dock, but he placed his knee on the rail ready to dive. Then he turned and stood with folded arms looking up to the bridge, for his mind was dark with many doubts. He tapped a passing sailor on the shoulder.

"What sort of an old boy is the captain?"

He made up his mind that according to the answer he would stay with the ship or swim to the shore, but the sailor merely stared stupidly at him for a moment and then grinned slowly. There might be malice, there might be mere ridicule in that smile. He passed on before another question could be asked.

"Huh!" grunted Harrigan. "I stay!"

He kept his eyes fixed on the bridge, remaining motionless at the rail for an hour while the glow of Honolulu grew dimmer and dimmer past the stern. There were lights in the after-cabin and he guessed that the ship, in a small way, carried both freight and passengers. At last McTee came down the steps to the deck and as he passed Harrigan snapped: "Follow me."

He led the way aft and up another flight of steps to the after-cabin, unlocked a door, and showed Harrigan into the captain's room. Here he took one chair and Harrigan dropped easily into another.

"Now, what 'n hell was your line of thinkin', McTee," he began, "when you told me to—"

"Stand up!" said McTee.

"What?"

"Stand up!"

Harrigan rose very slowly. His jaw was setting harder and harder, and his face became grim.

"Harrigan, you took a chance and came with me."

"Yes."

"I didn't ask you to come."

"Sure you didn't, but if you think you can treat me like a swine and get away with it—"

It was wonderful to see the eyes of McTee grow small. They seemed to retreat until they became points of light shining from the deep shadow of his brow. They were met by the cold, incurious light of Harrigan's stare.

"You're a hard man, Harrigan."

He made no answer, but listened to the deep thrum of the engines. It seemed to him that the force which drove the ship was like a part of McTee's will, a thing of steel.

"And I'm a hard man, Harrigan. On this ship I'm king. There's no will but my will; there's no right but my right; there's no law but my law. Remember, on land we stood as equals. On this ship you stand and I sit."

The thin lips did not curve, and yet they seemed to be smiling cruelly, and the eyes were probing deep, deep, deep into Harrigan's soul, weighing, measuring, searching.

"When we reach land," said Harrigan, "I got an idea I'll have to break you."

He raised his hands, which trembled with the restrained power of his arms, and moved them as though slowly breaking a stick of wood.

"I've broken men—like that," he finished.

"When I'm through with you, Harrigan, you'll take water from a Chinaman. You're the first man I've ever seen who could make me stop and look twice. I need a fellow like you, but first I've got to make you my man. The best colt in the world is no good until he learns to take the whip without bucking. I'm going to get you used to the whip. This is frank talk, eh? Well, I'm a frank man. You're in the harness now, Harrigan; make up your mind: Will you pull or will you balk? Answer me!"

"I'll see you damned!"

"Good. You've started to balk, so now you'll have to feel the whip."

He pulled a cord, and while they waited, the relentless duel of the eyes continued. A flash of instinct like a woman's intuition told Harrigan what impulse was moving McTee. He knew it was the same thing which makes the small schoolboy fight with the stranger; the same curiosity as to the unknown power, the same relentless will to be master, but now intensified a thousandfold in McTee, who looked for the first time, perhaps, on a man who might be his master. Harrigan knew, and smiled. He was confident. He half rejoiced in looking forward to the long struggle.

A knock came and the door opened.

"Masters," said McTee to the boatswain, "we're three hands short."

"Yes, sir."

"Here are the three hands. Take them forward."

CHAPTER 3

MASTERS LOOKED at Harrigan, started to laugh, looked again, and then silently held the door open. Harrigan stepped through it and followed to the forecastle, a dingy retreat in the high bow of the ship. He had to bend low to pass through the door, and inside he found that he could not stand erect. It was his first experience of working aboard a ship, and he expected to find a scrupulous neatness, and hammocks in place of beds. Instead he looked on a double row of bunks heaped with swarthy quilts, and the boatswain with a silent gesture indicated that one of these belonged to Harrigan. He went to it without a word and sat down cross-legged to survey his new quarters. It was more like the bunkhouse of a western ranch than anything else he had been in, but all reduced to a miniature, cramped and confined.

Now his eyes grew accustomed to the dim, unpleasant light which came from a single lantern hanging on the central post, and he began to make out the faces of the sailors. An oily-skinned Greek squatted on the bunk to his left. To his right was a Chinaman, marvelously emaciated; his lips pulled back in a continual smile, meaningless, like the grin of a corpse.

Opposite was the inevitable Englishman, slender, good-looking, with pale hair and bright, active eyes. Harrigan had traveled over half the world and never failed to find at least one subject of John Bull in any considerable group of men. This young fellow was talking with a giant Negro, his neighbor. The black man chattered with enthusiasm while the Englishman listened, nodding, intent.

One thing at least was certain about this crew: the Negro, the Chinaman, the Greek, even the Englishman, despite his slender build, they were all hard, strong men.

The cook brought out supper in buckets—stews, chunks of stale bread, tea. As they ate, the sailors grew talkative.

"Slide the slum this way," said the Englishman.

The Negro pushed the bucket across the deck with his foot.

"A hard trip," went on the first speaker.

"All trips on the *Mary Rogers* is hard," rumbled a voice.

"Aye, but Black McTee is blacker'n ever today."

"He belted the bos'n with a rope end," commented the Negro.

"He ain't human. This is my last trip with him. How about you, John? You got a lump on your jaw yet where he cracked you for breakin' that truck."

This was to the Chinaman, who answered in a soft guttural as if there were bubbling oil in his throat: "Me sail two year Black McTee, an'—"

To finish his speech he passed a tentative hand across his swollen jaw.

"And you'll sail with him till you die, John," said the Englishman. "When a man has had Black McTee for a boss, he'll want no other. He's to other captains what whisky is to beer."

The white teeth of the Negro showed. "Maybe Black McTee won't live long," he suggested.

There was a long silence. It lasted until the supper was finished. It lasted until the men slid into their bunks. And Harrigan knew that every man was repeating slowly to himself: "Maybe Black McTee won't live long."

"Not if this gang goes after him," muttered Harrigan, "and yet—"

He remembered the fight in Ivilei and the heaving shoulders which showed above the heads of the swarming soldiers. With that picture in his mind he went to sleep.

They were far out of sight of land in the morning and loafing south before the trade wind, with a heavy ground swell kicking them along from behind. Harrigan saw the *Mary Rogers* plainly for the first time. She was small, not more than fifteen hundred or two thousand tons, and the dingiest, sootiest of all tramp freighters. He had little time to make observations.

In the first place all hands washed down the decks, some of the men in rubber boots, the others barefooted, with their trousers rolled up above the knees. Harrigan was one of this number. The cool water from the hose swished pleasantly about his toes. He began to think better of life at sea as the wind blew from his nostrils the musty odors of the forecastle. Then the bos'n, with the suggestion of a grin in his eyes, ordered him up to scrub the bridge. He climbed the steps with a bucket in one hand and a brush in the other. There stood McTee leaning against the wheelhouse and staring straight ahead across the bows. He seemed quite oblivious of his presence until, having finished his job, Harrigan started back down the steps.

"D'you call this clean?" rumbled McTee. "All over again!"

And Harrigan dropped to his knees without protest and commenced scrubbing again. As he worked, he hummed a tune and saw the narrow jaw of McTee jut out. Harrigan smiled.

He had scarcely finished stowing his bucket and brush away when the bos'n brought him word that he was wanted in the fireroom. Masters's face was serious.

"What's the main idea?" asked Harrigan.

The bos'n cast a worried eye fore and aft.

"Black McTee's breakin' you," he said; "you're getting the whip."

"Well?"

"God help you, that's all. Now get below."

There was a certain fervency about this speech which impressed even Harrigan. He brooded over it on his way to the fireroom. There he was set to work passing coal. He had to stand in a narrow passage scarcely wide enough for him to turn about in. On either side was a towering black heap which slanted down to his feet. Midway between the piles was the little door through which he shoveled the coal into the fireroom.

All was stifling hot, with a breath of coal dust and smoke to choke the lungs. Even the Greek firemen sweated and cursed, though they were used to that environment. An ordinary man might have succumbed simply to that fiery, foul atmosphere. It was like a glimpse of hell, dark, hopeless.

It was not the heat or the atmosphere which troubled Harrigan, but his hands. His skin was puffed and soft from the scrubbing of the bridge. Now as he grasped the rough wood of the short-handled scoop the epidermis wore quickly and left his palms half raw. For a time he managed to shift his grip, bringing new portions of his hands to bear on the wood, but even this skin was worn away in time. When he finished his shift, his hands were bleeding in places and raw in the palms.

As he came on deck, he tied them up with bits of soft waste in lieu of a bandage and made no complaint, yet his fingers were trembling when he ate supper that night. He caught the eyes of the rest of the crew studying him with a cold calculation. They were estimating the strength of his endurance and he knew at once that they had been through the same trial one by one until they were broken.

He could see that they hated the captain and he wondered why they would ship with him time and again. He watched their expressions when Black McTee was mentioned, and then he understood. They were waiting for the time when the captain should weaken. Then they would have their revenge.

The second day was a repetition of the first. He began with scrubbing down the bridge. The suds, strong with lye, ate shrewdly at his raw hands. Still he hummed as he worked and watched McTee's frown grow dark. When he was ordered below to the fireroom, he wrapped his hands in the soft waste again. That helped him for a time, but after the first two hours the waste matted and grew hard with perspiration and blood. He had to throw it away and take the shovel handle against his bare skin. He told himself that it was only a matter of time before calluses would form, but what chance was there for a formation of calluses when the water and suds softened his hands every morning?

On the third day he was a little more used to the torture. His hands were hopelessly raw now, but still he made no complaint and stuck with his task. That night he secured a rag and retreated to the stretch of deck between the wheelhouse and the after-cabin, where he squatted beside a bucket of water and washed his hands carefully. Both hands were puffed and red; one of the creases in the left palm bled a steady trickle. He washed them slowly, with infinite relish of the cool water, until he felt that peculiar sensation which warns us that we are watched by another eye.

He looked up to see a young woman standing above him at the rail of the after-cabin. She had been watching him by the light from the window of the wheelhouse.

CHAPTER 4

"LET ME bandage your hands," she said. "I have some salve in my room."

Her voice was a balm to the troubled heart of Harrigan. His knotted forehead relaxed.

"Are you coming up?"

"Aye."

He ran up the ladder and followed her to a cabin. She rummaged through a suitcase and finally brought out a little tin box of salve and a roll of gauze. As she stooped with her back to him, he saw that her hair was red—not fiery red like his, but a deep dull bronze, with points of gold where the light struck it. When she straightened and turned, her eyes went wide, looking up to him, for he bulked huge in the tiny cabin.

"What a big fellow you are!"

He did not answer for a moment; he was too busy watching her eyes, which were sea-green, and strangely pleasant and restful.

"Do you know me?" she asked with a slight frown.

"'Scuse me," muttered Harrigan. "I thought at first I did."

He abased his glance while she took one of his hands and turned it palm up.

"Ugh!" she muttered. "How did this happen?"

"Work."

"Do you mean to say they make you work with your hands in this condition?"

"Sure."

"Poor fellow! That black captain!"

Her voice had changed from a peculiarly soft, low accent to a shrill tone that made Harrigan start.

"Poor fellow!" she repeated. "Sit down."

The campstool creaked under the burden of his weight. She pulled up the chair in front of him and placed his left hand on her knees.

"This is peroxide. Tell me if it hurts too much."

She spilled some of the liquid across his palm; it frothed.

"Ouch!" grunted Harrigan involuntarily.

She caught his wrists with both hands.

"Why, your whole arm is trembling! You must be in torture with this. Have you made any complaint?"

"No."

She studied him for a moment, scenting a mystery somewhere and guessing that he would not speak of it. And she asked no questions. She said not a word and merely bowed her head and started to apply the salve with delicate touches. For the result, a confession of all his troubles tumbled up the big man's throat to his tongue. He had to set his teeth to keep it back.

She became aware of those cold, incurious eyes studying her face as she wrapped the gauze bandage deftly around the injured palms.

"Why do you watch me so closely?"

It disarmed him. Those possibilities of tenderness came about his stiff-set lips, and the girl wondered.

"I was thinkin' about my home town."

"Where is it?"

He frowned and waved his hand in a sweep which included half the points on the compass.

"Back there."

She waited, wrapping up the gauze bandage.

"When I was a kid, I used to go down to the harbor an' watch the ships comin' in an' goin' out," he went on cautiously.

She nodded, and he resumed with more confidence: "I'd sit on the pierhead an' watch the ships. I knew they was bringing the smell of far lands in their holds."

There was a little pause; then his head tilted back and he burst into the soft, thick brogue: "Ah-h, I was afther bein' woild about the schooners blowin' out to sea wid their sails shook out like clouds. An' then I'd look down to the wather around the pier, an' it was green, deep green, ah-h, the deep sea-green av it! An' I would look into it an' dream. Whin I seen your eyes—"

16

He stopped, grown cold as a man will when he feels that he has laid his inner self indecently bare to the eye of the world. But she did not stir; she did not smile.

"I felt like a kid again," said Harrigan, recovering from the brogue. "Like a kid sittin' on the pierhead an' watchin' the green water. Your eyes are that green," he finished.

Self-consciousness, the very thing which she had been trying to keep the big sailor from, turned her blood to fire. She knew the quick color was running from throat to cheek; she knew the cold, incurious eye would note the change. He was so far aware of the alteration that he rose and glanced at the door.

"Good-by," she said, and then quite forgetting herself: "I shall ask the captain to see that you are treated like a white man."

"You will not!"

"I beg your pardon?" she said, but the hint of insulted dignity was lost on Harrigan.

"You will not," he repeated. "It'd simply make him worse."

She was glad of the chance to be angry; it would explain her heightening color.

"The captain must be an utter brute."

"I figger he's nine tenths man, an' the other tenth devil, but there ain't no human bein' can change any of them ten parts. Good-by. I'm thankin' you. My name's Harrigan."

She opened the door for him.

"If you wish to have that dressing changed, ask for Miss Malone."

"Ah-h!" said Harrigan. "Malone!"

She explained coldly: "I'm Scotch, not Irish."

"Scotch or Irish," said Harrigan, and his head tilted back as it always did when he was excited. "You're afther bein' a real shport, Miss Malone!"

"Miss Malone," she repeated, closing the door after him, and vainly attempting to imitate the thrill which he gave to the word. "What a man!"

She smiled for a moment into space and then pulled the cord for the cabin boy.

CHAPTER 5

THE CABIN boy did duty for all the dozen passengers, and therefore he was slow in answering. When he appeared, she asked him to carry the captain word that she wished to speak with him. He returned in a short time to say that Captain McTee would talk with her now in his cabin. She followed aft to the captain's room. He did not rise when she entered, but turned in his chair and relinquished a long, black, fragrant cigar.

"Don't stop smoking," she said. "I want you in a pleasant mood to hear what I have to say."

Without reply he placed the cigar in his mouth and the bright black eyes fastened upon her. That suddenly intent regard was startling, as if he had leaned over and spoken a word in her ear. She shrugged her shoulders as if trying to shake off a compelling hand and then settled into a chair.

"I've come to say something that's disagreeable for you to hear and for me to speak."

Still he would not talk. He was as silent as Harrigan. She clenched her hands and drove bravely ahead. She told how she had called the red-headed sailor up to the after-cabin and dressed his hurts, and she described succinctly, but with rising anger the raw and swollen condition of his fingers. The captain listened with apparent enjoyment; she could not tell whether he was relishing her story or his slowly puffed cigar. In the end she waited for his answer, but evidently none was forthcoming.

"Now," she said at last, "I know something about ships and sailors, and I know that if this fellow was to appeal against you after you touch port, a judge would weigh a single word of yours against a whole sentence of Harrigan's. It would be a different matter if a disinterested person pressed a charge of cruelty against you. I am such a person; I would press such a charge; I have the money, the time, and the inclination to do it."

She read the slight hesitation in his manner, not as if he were impressed by what she had to say, but as though he was questioning himself as to whether he should give her any answer at all. It made her wish fervently that she were a man—and a big one. He spoke then, as if an illuminating thought had occurred to him.

"You know Harrigan's record?"

"No," she admitted grudgingly.

McTee sighed as if with deep relief and leaned back in his chair. His smile was sympathetic and it altered his face so marvelously that she caught her breath.

"Of course that explains it, Miss Malone. I don't doubt that he was clever enough to make you think him abused."

"He didn't say a word of accusation against anyone."

"Naturally not. When a man is bad enough to seem honest—"

He drew a long, slow puff on his cigar by way of finishing his sentence and his eyes smiled kindly upon her.

"I knew that he would do his worst to start mutiny among the crew; I didn't think he could get as far as the passengers."

Her confidence was shaken to the ground. Then a new suspicion came to her.

"If he is such a terrible character, why did you let him come aboard your ship?"

Instead of answering, he pulled a cord. The bos'n appeared in a moment.

"Tell this lady how Harrigan came aboard," ordered the captain, and he fastened a keen eye upon the bos'n.

"Made it on the jump while we was pullin' out of dock," said the sailor. "Just managed to get his feet on the gangplank—came within an ace of falling into the sea."

"That's all."

The bos'n retreated and McTee turned back to Kate Malone.

"He had asked me to sign him up for this trip," he explained. "If I'd set him ashore, he'd probably have been in the police court the next morning. So I let him stay. To be perfectly frank with you, I had a vague hope that gratitude might make a decent sailor out of him for a few days. But the very first night he started his work he began to talk discontent among the men in the forecastle, and such fellows are always ready to listen. Of course I could throw Harrigan in irons and feed him on bread and water; my authority is absolute at sea. But I don't want to do that if I can help it. Instead, I have been trying to discipline him with hard work. He knows that he can come to me at any time and speak three words which will release him from his troubles. But he won't say them—yet!"

"Really?" she breathed.

She began to feel deeply honored that such a man as McTee would make so long an explanation to her.

"Shall I call him up here and ask him to say them now?"

"Would you do that? Captain McTee, I'm afraid that I've been very foolish to bother you in this matter, but—"

He silenced her with a wave of the hand, and pulled the cord.

"Bring up Harrigan," he said, when the bos'n appeared again.

"I've considered myself a judge of human nature," she apologized, "but I shall think a long time before I venture another decision."

"You're wrong to feel that way. It would take a shrewd judge to see through Harrigan unless his record were known."

The door opened and the bos'n entered with Harrigan. He fixed his eyes upon the captain without a glance for Kate Malone.

"Harrigan," said McTee, "I've been telling Miss Malone that you can be released from your trouble by saying half a dozen words to me. And you know that you can. You will be treated better than anyone in the crew if you will put your hand in mine and say: 'Captain McTee, I give you my word of honor as a man to do my best to obey orders during the rest of this trip and to hold no malice against you for anything that has happened to me so far.'

"For you see," he explained to the girl, "he probably thinks himself aggrieved by my discipline. Will you say it, Harrigan?"

Instead of answering, the cold eye of Harrigan turned on Kate.

"I told you not to speak to the captain," he said.

"Ah," said McTee, "you were clever enough for that?"

"Do you say nothing, Harrigan?" she said incredulously. "Do you really refuse to speak those words to the captain after he has been generous enough to give you a last chance to make a man of yourself?"

Harrigan turned pale as he glanced at the captain. Her scorn and contempt gave a little metallic ring to her voice.

"You need not be afraid. Captain McTee hasn't told me anything about your record."

Harrigan smiled, but in such a manner that she stepped back. "Easy," said McTee, "you don't need to fear him in here. He knows that I'm his master."

"I'm glad you didn't tell me his record," she answered.

"I can read it in his eyes."

"Lady," said Harrigan, and his head tilted back till the cords stood strongly out at the base of his throat, "I'm afther askin' your pardon for thinkin' ye had ever a dr-rop av hot Irish blood in ye."

"Take him below, bos'n," broke in McTee, "and put him in on the night shift in the fireroom."

No hours of Harrigan's life were bitterer than that night shift. The bandages saved his hands from much of the torture of the shovel handle, but there was deep night in his heart. Early in the morning one of the firemen ran to the chief engineer's room and forced open the door.

"The red-headed man, sir," he stammered breathlessly.

The chief engineer awoke with a snarl. He had drunk much good Scotch whisky that evening, and the smoke of it was still dry in his throat and cloudy in his brain.

"And what the hell is wrong with the red-headed man now?" he roared. "Ain't he doin' two men's work still?"

"Two? He's doin' ten men's work with his hands rolled in cloth and the blood soakin' through, an' he sings like a devil while he works. He's gone crazy, sir."

"Naw, he ain't," growled the chief; "that'll come later. Black McTee is breakin' him an' he'll be broke before he goes off his nut. Now get to hell out of here. I ain't slept a wink for ten days."

The fireman went back to his work muttering, and Harrigan sang the rest of the night.

CHAPTER 6

IN THE morning there was the usual task of scrubbing down the bridge. The suds soaked through the bandages at once and burned his hands like fire. He tore away the cloths and kept at his task, for he knew that if he refused to continue, he became by that act of disobedience a mutineer.

The fourth day was a long nightmare, but at the end of it Harrigan was still at his post. That night the pain kept him awake. For forty-eight hours he had not closed his eyes. The next morning, as he prepared his bucket of suds and looked down at his blood-caked hands, the thought of surrender rose strongly for the first time. Two things fought against it: his fierce pride and a certain awe which he had noted as it grew from day to day in the eyes of the rest of the crew. They were following the silent battle between the great Irishman and the captain with a profound, an almost uncanny interest.

As he scrubbed the bridge that morning, McTee, as always, stood staring out across the bows, impassive, self-contained as a general overlooking a field of battle. And the temptation to surrender swelled up in the throat of Harrigan like the desire for speech in a child. He kept his teeth hard together and prayed for endurance. Only five days, and it might be weeks before they made a port. Even then the captain might put him in irons rather than risk his escape.

"Harrigan," said McTee suddenly. "Don't keep it up. You're bound to break. Speak those words now that I told you to say and you're a free man."

Harrigan looked up and the words formed at the base of his tongue. Harrigan looked down and saw his crimson hands. The words fell back like dust on his heart.

"Take you for my master an' swear to forget what you've done?" he said, and his voice was hardly more than a whisper. "McTee, if I promised you that I'd perjure blacker 'n hell an' kill you someday when your back was turned. As it is, I'll kill you while we're standin' face to face."

McTee laughed, low, deep, and his eyes were half closed as if he heard pleasant music. Harrigan grinned up at him.

"I'll kill you with my bare hands. There's no gun or knife could do justice to what's inside of me."

His head tilted back and his whisper went thick like that of a drunkard: "Ahh, McTee, look at the hands, look at the hands! They're red now for a sign av the blood av ye that'll someday be on 'em!"

And he picked up his bucket and brush and went down the deck. The laugh of McTee followed him.

Having framed the wish in words, it was never absent from Harrigan's mind now. It made that day easier for him. He stopped singing. He needed all his brain energy to think of how he should kill McTee.

It was this hungry desire which sustained him during the days which followed. The rest of the crew began to sense the mighty emotion which consumed Harrigan. When they saw both him and McTee on the deck, their eyes traveled from one to the other making comparisons, for they felt that these men would one day meet hand to hand. They could not stay apart any more than the iron can keep from the magnet.

Finally Harrigan knew that they were nearing the end of their long journey. The port was only a few days distant, for they were far in the south seas and they began to pass islands, and sometimes caught sight of green patches of water. Those were the coral reefs, the terror of all navigators, for they grow and change from year to year. To a light-draught ship like the *Mary Rogers* these seas were comparatively safe, but not altogether. Even small sailing craft had come to grief in those regions.

Yet the islands, the reefs, the keen sun, the soft winds, the singing of the sailors, all these things came dimly to Harrigan, for he knew that his powers of resistance were almost worn away. His face was a mask of tragedy, and his body was as lean as a starved wolf in winter. His will to live, his will to hate, alone remained.

Each morning it was harder for him to leave the bridge without speaking those words to the captain. He rehearsed them every day and vowed they would never pass his lips. And every day he knew that his vow was weaker. When he was about to give in, he chanced to see McTee and Kate Malone laughing together on the promenade.

It was McTee who saw Harrigan first and pointed him out to Kate. She leaned against the rail and peered down at him, shuddering at the sight of his drawn face and shadowed eyes. Then she turned with a little shrug of repulsion.

McTee must have made some humorous comment, for she turned to glance down at Harrigan again and this time she laughed. Blind rage made the blood of the Irishman hot. That gave him his last strength, but even this ran out. Finally he knew that the next day was his last, and when that day came, he counted the hours. They passed heavy-footed, as time goes for one condemned to die. And then he sat cross-legged on his bunk and waited.

The giant Negro came, bringing word that the bos'n wanted him to scrub down the bridge. He remained with his head bowed, unhearing. The bos'n himself came, cursing. He called to Harrigan, and getting no answer shook him by the shoulder. He put his hand under Harrigan's chin and raised the listless head. It rolled heavily back and the dull eyes stared up at him.

"God!" said the bos'n, and started back.

The head remained where he had placed it, the eyes staring straight up at the ceiling.

"God!" whispered the bos'n again, and ran from the forecastle.

In time—it seemed hours—Harrigan heard many voices approaching. McTee's bass was not among them, but he knew that McTee was coming, and Harrigan wondered whether he would have the strength to refuse to obey and accept the fate of the mutineer; or whether terror would overwhelm him and he would drop to his knees and beg for mercy. He had once seen a sight as horrible. The voices swept closer. McTee was bringing all the available crew to watch the surrender, and Harrigan prayed with all his soul to a nameless deity for strength.

Something stopped in the Irishman. It was not his heart, but something as vital. The very movement of the earth seemed to be suspended when the great form blocked the door to the forecastle and the ringing voice called: "Harrigan!"

At the summons Harrigan's jaw fell loosely like that of an exhausted distance-runner, and long-suppressed words grew achingly large in his throat.

"I've had enough!" he groaned.

"Harrigan!" thundered the captain, and Harrigan knew that his attempted speech had been merely a silent wish.

"God help me!" he whispered hoarsely, and in response to that brief prayer a warm pulse of strength flooded through him. He sprang to his feet.

"I refuse to work!" he cried, and this time the sound echoed back against his ears.

There was a long pause.

"Mutiny!" said McTee at last, and his voice was harsh with the knowledge of his failure. "Bring him outside in the open. I'll deal with him!"

He retreated from the door, but before any of the sailors could go in to fulfill the order, Harrigan walked of his own accord out onto the deck. The wind on his face was sweet and keen; the vapors blew from eyes and brain. He was himself again, weaker, but himself. He saw the circle of wondering, awe-stricken faces; he saw McTee standing with folded arms.

CHAPTER 7

"MUTINY ON the high seas," the captain was saying, "is as bad as murder on dry land. I could swing you by the neck from the mast for this, Harrigan, and every court would uphold me. Or I can throw you into the irons and leave your trial until we touch port. But—stand back!"

At the wave of his hand the circle spread. McTee stepped close to Harrigan.

"I could do all that I've said, but why should I waste you on a prison when there's a chance that I can use for myself? Harrigan, will you stand up to me, man to man, and fist to fist, fighting fair and square without advantage, and then if I thrash you, will you be my man? If I beat you, will you swear to follow me, to do my bidding? Harrigan, if I have you to work for me—I'll be king of the south seas!"

"Man to man—fair and square?" repeated Harrigan vaguely. "I'm weak. You've had me in hell an' sweated me thin, McTee. If I was my old self, I'd jump at the chance."

"Then it's irons for you and ten years for mutiny when we reach port."

"Ah-h, damn your heart!"

"But if I beat you, you'll be a lord of men, Harrigan, with only one king over you—McTee! You'll live on the fat of the land and the plunder of the high seas if you serve McTee."

"What oath could I swear that you'd believe?"

"Your hand in mind for a pledge—I ask no more."

He held out his hand. The lean, strong fingers fascinated Harrigan.

"I'd rather take your throat than your hand, McTee—an' mebbe I will—an' mebbe I will!"

He caught the hand in his own cracked, stained, black palm. The smile of McTee was like the smile of Satan when he watched Adam driven from the Eden.

"Strip to the waist," he said, and turned on the crew.

"You know me, lads. I've tried to break Harrigan, but I've only bent him, and now he's going to stand up to me man to man, and if he wins, he's free to do as he likes and never lift a hand till we reach port. Aye, lick your chops, you dogs. There's none of you had the heart to try what Harrigan is going to try."

If they did not actually lick their chops, there was hunger in their eyes and a strange wistfulness as they watched Harrigan strip off his shirt, but when they saw the wasted arms, lean, with the muscles defined and corded as if by famine,

23

their faces went blank again. For they glanced in turn at the vast torso of McTee. When he moved his arms, his smooth shoulders rippled in significant spots—the spots where the driving muscles lay. But Harrigan saw nothing save the throat of which he had dreamed.

"This is to the finish?" said McTee.

"Aye."

"And no quarter?"

Harrigan grinned, and slipped out to the middle of the deck. Both of them kicked off their shoes. Even in their bare feet it would be difficult to keep upright, for the *Mary Rogers* was rollicking through a choppy sea. Harrigan sensed the crew standing in a loose circle with the hunger of the wolf pack in winter stamped in their eyes.

McTee stood with his feet braced strongly, his hands poised. But Harrigan stole about him with a gliding, unequal step. He did not seem preparing to strike with his hands, which hung low, but rather like one who would leap at the throat with his teeth. The ship heaved and Harrigan sprang and his fists cracked—one, two. He leaped out again under the captain's clubbed hands. Two spots of red glowed on McTee's ribs and the wolf pack moistened their lips.

"Come again, Harrigan, for I've smelled the meat, not tasted it."

"It tastes red—like this."

And feinting at McTee's body, he suddenly straightened and smashed both hands against the captain's mouth. McTee's head jarred back under the impact. The wolf pack murmured. The captain made a long step, waited until Harrigan had leaped back to the side of the deck to avoid the plunge, and then, as the deck heaved up to give added impetus to his lunge, he rushed. The angle of the deck kept the Irishman from taking advantage of his agility. He could not escape. One pile-driver hand cracked against his forehead—another thudded on his ribs. He leaped through a shower of blows and clinched.

He was crushed against the rail. He was shaken by a quick succession of short arm punches. But anything was preferable to another of those long, driving blows. He clung until his head cleared. Then he shook himself loose and dropped, as if dazed, to one knee. McTee's bellow of triumph filled his ears. The captain bore down on him with outstretched hands to grapple at his throat, but at the right instant Harrigan rose and lurched out with stiff arm. The punch drove home to the face with a shock that jarred Harrigan to his feet and jerked McTee back as if drawn by a hand. Before he recovered his balance, Harrigan planted half a dozen punches, but though they shook the captain, they did not send him down, and Harrigan groaned.

McTee bellowed again. It was not pain. It was not mere rage. It was a battle cry, and with it he rushed Harrigan. They raged back and forth across the deck, and the wolf pack drew close, cursing beneath their breath. They had looked for a quick end to the struggle, but now they saw that the fighters were mated. The greater strength was McTee's; the greater purpose was Harrigan's. McTee fought to crush and conquer; Harrigan fought to kill.

The blows of the captain flung Harrigan here and there, yet he came back to meet the attack, slinking with sure, catlike steps. The heel and pitch of the deck sometimes staggered the captain, but Harrigan seemed to know beforehand what would happen, and he leaped in at every opening with blows that cut the skin.

His own flesh was bruised. He bled from mouth and nose, but what was any other pain compared with the torture of his clenched fists? It made his arms numb to the elbow and sent currents of fire through his veins. His eyes kept on the thick throat of McTee. Though he was knocked reeling and half senseless, his stare never changed, and the wolf pack, with their heads jutting forward with eagerness watched, waited. The "Ha!" of McTee rang with the strength of five throats. The "Wah-h!" of Harrigan purred like a furious panther's snarl.

Then as the frenzy left Harrigan and the numbness departed from his arms, he knew that he was growing weaker and weaker. In McTee's eyes he saw the growing light of victory, the confidence. His own wild hunger for blood grew apace with his desperation. He flung himself forward in a last effort.

A ponderous fist cracked home between his eyes, fairly lifting him from his feet and hurling him against the base of the wheelhouse. Then a forearm shot under his shoulder and a hand fastened on the back of his neck in an incomplete half-Nelson. As McTee applied the pressure, Harrigan felt his vertebral column give under the tremendous strain. He struggled furiously but could not break the grip. Far away, like the storm wind in the forest, he heard the moan of the wolf pack.

"Give in! Give in!" panted McTee.

"Ah-h!" snarled Harrigan.

He felt the deck swing and jerked his legs high in the air. He could not have broken that grip of his own strength, but the sway of the deck gave his movement a mighty leverage. The hand slipped from his neck, scraping skin away, as if a red-hot iron had been drawn across the flesh. But he was half loosed, and that twist of his body sent them both rolling one over the other to the scuppers of the ship—and it was McTee who crashed against the rail, receiving the blow on the back of his head. His eyes went dull; the red hands of Harrigan fastened on his throat.

"God!" screamed McTee, and gripped Harrigan's wrists, but the Irishman heaved him up and beat his head against the deck.

McTee's jaws fell open, and a bloody froth bubbled to his lips; his eyes thrust out hideously.

"Ah-h!" snarled Harrigan, and shifted his grip lower, his thumbs digging relentlessly into the great throat. This time the giant limbs of the captain relaxed as if in sleep. Then through the fierce singing in his ears the Irishman heard a yell. He turned his head. The wolf pack saw their prey pulled down at last. They ran now to join the kill, not men, but raging devils. Harrigan sprang to his feet, catching up a marlinspike, and whirled it above his head.

"Back!" he shouted.

They shrank back, growling one to the other savagely, irresolute. There came a moan at Harrigan's feet. He leaned over and lifted the bulk of the captain's inert body. As if through a haze he saw the chief engineer and the two mates running toward him and caught the glitter of a revolver in the hands of the first officer. The Irishman's battered lips stretched to a shapeless grin.

"Help me to the captain's cabin," he said. "He's afther bein' sick."

CHAPTER 8

AND THE four of them went aft carrying McTee's body. On the promenade they passed Kate Malone. She shrank against the rail, her eyes blank and her face white.

"He's dead!" she cried.

"He's just beginnin' to live," said Harrigan.

The captain was muttering faintly as they laid him on the bunk in his room. "Now get out," commanded Harrigan. "I will be alone with him when he wakes up. I have something to whisper in his ear."

"Is it safe?" said the first mate to the chief engineer, gesturing with his weapon.

Harrigan snatched it away and waved it like a club above his head.

"Get out, or I'll bash your skull in."

His face was hideous, cut and blood-stained, starved with the long hunger and lighted with the victory. They slunk from the cabin, backing out as if they expected him to rush them. Harrigan locked the door and started to tend the captain. He washed McTee to the waist, cleansed the cut places carefully, and covered them with narrow strips of adhesive tape which he found in a small medicine chest. As the heavier breathing of the captain indicated that he was about to recover his senses, Harrigan performed the same services for himself. It was slow work, for now that the stimulus of action was gone, his weakness grew on him in recurrent waves. Finally a sound made him turn to see McTee propping himself up on the bunk with one elbow; his eyes, unconfused and steady, looked brightly out at Harrigan.

"You beat me?"

"It was the swing of the deck that rolled you over and broke your grip. I've stayed to tell you that."

"Chances or no chances, you beat me."

"Man, you'd have busted my back if it hadn't been for that buck of the ship. When your hand came away, it took the skin with it."

"And that's why you didn't finish me?"

"Aye."

"You'll never have the chance again."

"I want no chances; I want no help except my own strength as it was before you withered me with your hellfire."

"When we stand up again, I'll kill you, Harrigan."

"When we stand up again, I'll break you, Black McTee—like a rotten stick."

"Lie down here," said the captain, rising quickly. "You're sick."

He forced Harrigan onto the bunk and stretched him out at full length. The Irishman clenched his hands and fought against the sleep which crept over his senses.

"There's fire in my brain," muttered Harrigan, "an' it's trying to burn its way out."

McTee dipped a towel in cool water.

"I kept the rest of them away," went on the Irishman. "When you woke up, I wanted you to hear why I didn't finish you."

He raised his shaking hands and gripped at the air.

"Ah-h! When me ould silf is back, I'll shtand up to ye. Tis a promise, McTee. Black McTee, Black McTee—I'll make ye Red McTee—red as the palms av me hands."

McTee tied the cold, wet towel around Harrigan's forehead.

"I'll kill you by inches, Harrigan. You'll read hell in my eyes before your end. Drink this!"

He raised Harrigan's almost lifeless head and forced the neck of a whisky bottle between his teeth.

"Ah-h!" said Harrigan, blinking and coughing after the strong liquor had burned its way down his throat. "The feel av your throat under me thumbs was sweeter than the touch av a colleen's hand, McTee! I'm dead for shlape!"

And instantly his eyes closed; his breathing was deep and sonorous. The captain watched him for a long moment, then sat down and laying a hand on the sleeping man's wrist, he counted the pulse carefully. It was irregular and feeble.

"Time is all he needs," muttered McTee to himself, and he sat staring before him, dreaming. "A fool can live well," he was thinking, "but it takes a great man to die well. Harrigan will make a fine death." In the meantime the big Irishman slept heavily, and Black McTee tended him well, keeping the towel cool and wet about his forehead. The pulse was gaining rapidly in strength and regularity; sleep seemed to act upon Harrigan as food acts upon a starved man. At times he smiled, and McTee could guess at the dream which caused it. He was dreaming of killing McTee, and McTee sat by and understood, and smiled with deep content. He, also, was tasting his thoughts of the battle-to-be when, without any warning rap, the door swung open and the burly form of Bos'n Masters appeared.

"The first mate—" he began.

"Did you knock?"

"I've got no time to waste, the first mate—"

McTee rose. In the frank, bold eyes of the bos'n he read the open revolt, and understood. He had been beaten in open battle; his crew felt that they were liberated by the victory of their champion.

"Who told you to enter without knocking?" he broke in.

"I don't need telling," said the dauntless bos'n. "The first mate's drunk an'—"

The heavy fist of McTee landed on Masters's mouth and hurled him in a heap into the corner of the cabin. The captain seized him by the nape of the neck and jerked him back to his feet, blinking and gasping, thoroughly subdued.

"Get out and come in as you should."

The bos'n fled. A moment later a timid knock came at the door and McTee bade him enter. He stepped in, cap in hand, his eyes on the floor.

"The first mate's drunk, sir, an' runnin' amuck with the ship. He's at the wheel an' he won't leave it. We've nearly scraped one reef already. You know this ain't any open sea, sir. There's green water everywhere."

"Go up and give the fool my orders. Tell the second officer to take the wheel."

The bos'n retreated, but he returned within a few moments.

"He won't leave the wheel," he reported. "He said you could take your orders to the devil, sir."

"I'll tie him to the deck and skin him alive," said McTee calmly. "Stay here and watch Harrigan while I—"

He was jerked from his feet and hurled across the room, crashing against the cabin wall. When his senses returned, he was sitting on the floor staring stupidly into the white face of the bos'n, who was in a similar posture. Harrigan, who had been flung from the bunk, staggered to his feet.

"What the deuce is up?" asked the Irishman.

A chorus of piercing yells rose in answer from the deck outside.

"The end of the *Mary Rogers* ," said McTee. "Stay with me, Harrigan."

He caught the latter by the arm and dragged him out onto the deck. The hull of the ship at the bow must have been literally ripped away by the impact against the reef; already the deck sloped sharply to the bows.

McTee raised a voice that rang like a trumpet over the clamor as he gave his orders to clear away the boats. If he had been a moment earlier, he might have succeeded in getting at least one of them safely launched, but now the *Mary Rogers* was settling to her doom with a speed which made the crew senseless with terror. A half-gale which promised to swell soon into a veritable hurricane seemed to be lifting the freighter by the heel and driving her nose into the sea. The quick settling twilight of the tropics made the waters doubly cold and dark.

Not till the bows of the *Mary Rogers* were deep below the waves and her propeller humming loudly in the air did the captain desist from his efforts to bring order out of the panic of the crew. Half a dozen men, with the Chinaman at their head, had cut one boat from its davits, but plunging into it before it fairly struck the water, they tipped it far to one side. It filled instantly and sank, leaving its occupants struggling on the surface. The Chinaman, who apparently could not swim, gave up the struggle at once. He threw his clutching hands high above his head and went down; his scream was the first death cry of the wreck of the *Mary Rogers* .

McTee, with Harrigan at his heels, rushed for the second lifeboat. Under the directions of the captain, pointed and emphasized by blows of his fist, the boat was swung safely from the davits and lowered to the sea. The instant that it rode the waves, bouncing up and down on the choppy surface, the crew began leaping in, the drunken mate being the first overside.

The lifeboat was loaded from stem to stern, and only Harrigan, McTee, and half a dozen more remained on the ship when the boat swung a dozen feet away from the *Mary Rogers* and with the next wave was picked up and smashed against the freighter. Its side went in like a matchbox pressed by a strong thumb, and it zigzagged quickly below the surface. The yells of the swimmers rose in a long wail. McTee caught Harrigan by the shoulder and shouted in his ear: "Stay close and do what I do."

"Miss Malone!" yelled Harrigan in answer, and pointed.

She stood by the after-cabin, clinging to the rail with one hand while she attempted to adjust a life preserver with the other. The *Mary Rogers* lurched forward, a long slide that buried half of the ship under the sea. A giant wave towered above the side and licked the wheelhouse away.

"Let her go!" roared McTee. "Save ourselves and let her go."

It was a matter of seconds now before the last of the *Mary Rogers* should disappear. They clambered up to the after-cabin.

"For the love av God, McTee, she's a woman!"

The Irishman struggled up the deck toward the girl, but the captain caught him and held him fast.

"There's one chance," shouted Black McTee, and he pointed to the litter of the wrecked wheelhouse which tossed on the waves. "Overboard and make for a big timber."

But the eyes of Harrigan held on the form of the girl. They could only make out the shadow of her form with her hair blowing wildly on the wind. Then as swift as the sway of a bird's wing, a mass of black water tossed over the side of the *Mary Rogers* . When it was gone, the shadowy figure of the girl had disappeared with it.

"Now!" thundered McTee.

"Aye," said Harrigan.

CHAPTER 9

THEY CLIMBED the rail. Plainly Harrigan had made them delay too long, for now they had not time to swim beyond the reach of the swirl that would form when the ship went down. The *Mary Rogers* lurched to her grave as they sprang from the rail. A wave caught them and washed them beyond the grip of the whirlpool; another wave swung them back, and the waters sucked them down. Such was the force of that downward pull that it seemed to Harrigan as if a weight were attached to either foot. He drew a great, gasping breath before his head went under and then struck out with all his might.

When his lungs seemed bursting with the labor, he whirled to the surface again and drew another gasping breath. The storm had torn a rift in the clouds and through it looked the moon as if some god were peering through the curtain of mist to watch the havoc he was working. By this light Harrigan saw that he was being drawn down in a narrowing circle. Straight before him loomed a black fragment of the wreckage. He tried to swing to one side, but the current of the water bore him on. He received a heavy blow on the head and his senses went out like a snuffed light.

When consciousness returned, there was a sharp pain in both head and right shoulder, for it was on his shoulder that McTee had fastened his grip. The captain sprawled on a great timber, clutching it with both legs and one arm. With the free hand he held Harrigan. All this the Irishman saw by the haggard moonlight. Then they were pitched high up on the crest of a wave. As Harrigan grappled the timber with arms and legs, it turned over and over and then pitched down through empty space. The wind had literally cut away the top of the wave. He went down, submerged, and then rose to a giddy height again. As he caught a great breath of air, he saw that McTee was no longer on the timber.

A shout reached him, the sound being cut off in the middle by the noise of the wind and waves. He saw McTee a dozen feet away, swimming furiously. He came almost close enough to touch the timber with his hands, and then a twist of the wave separated them. Harrigan worked down the timber until he reached the end of the stanchion which was nearest Black McTee. All that time the captain was struggling, but could not draw closer. The wood was drifting before the wind faster than he could swim.

When he reached the end of the timber, Harrigan wound his long arms tightly around it and let his legs draw out on the water. McTee, seeing the purpose of the maneuver, redoubled his efforts. On a wave crest the storm swept Harrigan still farther away; then they dropped into a hollow and instantly he felt a mighty grip fall on his ankle. They pitched up again with the surge of a wave so sharp and sudden that what with his own weight and the tugging burden of McTee behind him, Harrigan felt as if his arms would be torn from their sockets. He kept his hold by a mighty effort, and the tremendous grip of McTee held fast on his ankle until they dropped once more into a hollow. Then the captain jerked himself hand over hand up the body of Harrigan until he reached the timber. They lay panting and exhausted on the stanchion, embracing it with arms and legs.

Sometimes the wind sent the timber with its human freight lunging through a towering wave; and several times the force of the storm caught them and whirled them over and over. When they rose to a wave crest, they struggled bitterly for life; when they fell into the trough, they drew long breaths and freshened their holds.

Save once when Harrigan reached out his hand and set it upon that of Black McTee. The captain met the grip, and by the wild moonlight they stared into each other's faces. That handshake almost cost them their lives, for the next moment the full breath of the storm caught them and wrenched furiously at their bodies. Yet neither of them regretted the handclasp, for all its cost. If they died now, it would be as brothers. They had at least escaped from the greatest of all horrors, a lonely death.

It seemed as if the storm acknowledged the strength of their determination. It fell away as suddenly as it had risen. A heavy ground swell still ran, but without the wind to roughen the surface and sharpen the crests, the big timber rode safely through the sea. The storm clouds were dropping back in a widening circle beneath the moon when, as they heaved up on the top of a wave, Harrigan suddenly pointed straight ahead and shouted hoarsely. On the horizon squatted a black shadow, darker than any cloud.

All night they watched the shadow grow, and when the morning came and the tropic dawn stepped suddenly up from the east, the light glinted on the un-mistakable green of verdure.

With the help of the steady wind they drifted slowly closer and closer to the island. By noon they abandoned the timber and started swimming, but the submerged beach went out far more gradually than they had expected. The last hundred yards they walked arm in arm, floundering through the gentle surf.

Then they stumbled up the beach, reeling with weariness, and sprawled out in the shade of a palm tree. They were asleep almost before they struck the sand.

It was late afternoon when they woke, ravenously hungry, their throats burning with thirst. For food McTee climbed a coconut palm and knocked down some of the fruit. They split the gourds open on a rock, drank the liquor, and ate heartily of the meat. That quelled their appetites, but the sweet liquor only partially appeased their thirst, and they started to search the island for a spring. First they went to the center of the place to a small hill, and from the top of this they surveyed their domain. The island was not more than a thousand yards in width and three or four miles in length. Nowhere was there any sign of even a hut.

"Well?" queried Harrigan, seeing McTee frown.

"We can live here," explained the captain, "but God knows how long it will be before we sight a ship. Our only hope is for some tramp freighter that's trying to find a short cut through the reefs. Even if we sight a tramp, how'll we signal her?"

"With a fire."

"Aye, if one passes at night. We could stack up wood on the top of this hill. The island isn't charted. If a skipper saw a light, he might take a chance and send a boat. But how could we kindle a fire?"

They went slowly down the hill, their heads bent. At the base, as if placed in their path to cheer them in this moment of gloom, they found a spring. It ran a dozen feet and disappeared into a crevice. They cupped the water in their hands and drank long and deep. When they stood up again, McTee dropped a hand on Harrigan's shoulder. He said: "You've cause enough for hating me."

"Pal," said Harrigan, "you're nine parts devil, but the part of you that's a man makes up for all the rest."

McTee brooded: "Now we're standing on the rim of the world, and we've got to be brother to each other. But what if we get off the island—there's small chance of it, but what if we should? Would we remember then how we took hands in the trough of the sea?"

Harrigan raised his hand.

"So help me God—" he began.

"Wait!" broke in McTee. "Don't say it. Suppose we get off the island, and when we reach port find one thing which we both want. What then?"

Harrigan remembered a word from the Bible.

"I'll never covet one of your belongin's, McTee, an' I'll never cross your wishes."

"Your hair is red, Harrigan, and mine is black; your eye is blue and mine is black. We were made to want the same thing in different ways. I've never met my mate before. I can stand it here on the rim of the world—but in the world itself—what then, Harrigan?"

They stepped apart, and the glance of the black eye crossed that of the cold blue.

"Ah-h, McTee, are ye dark inside and out? Is the black av your eye the same as the soot in your heart?"

"Harrigan, you were born to fight and forget; I was born to fight and remember. Well, I take no oath, but here's my hand. It's better than the oath of most men."

"A strange fist," grinned Harrigan; "soft in the palm and hard over the knuckles—like mine."

They went down the hill toward the beach, Harrigan singing and McTee silent, with downward head. On the beach they started for some rocks which shelved out into the water, for it was possible that they might find some sort of shellfish on the rocks below the surface of the water. Before they reached the place, however, McTee stopped and pointed out across the waves. Some object tossed slowly up and down a short distance from the beach.

"From the wreck," said McTee. "I didn't think it would drift quite as fast as this."

They waded out to examine; the water was not over their waists when they reached it. They found a whole section from the side of the wheelhouse, the timbers intact.

On it lay Kate Malone, unconscious.

Manifestly she never could have kept on the big fragment during the night of the storm had it not been for a piece of stout twine with which she had tied her left wrist to a projecting bolt. She had wrapped the cord many times, but despite this it had worn away her skin and sunk deep in the flesh of her arm. Half her clothes were torn away as she had been thrown about on the boards. Whether from exhaustion or the pain of her cut wrist, she had fainted and evidently lain in this position for several hours; one side of her face was burned pink by the heat of the sun.

They dragged the float in, and McTee knelt beside the girl and pressed an ear against her breast.

"Living!" he announced. "Now we're three on the rim of the world."

"Which makes a crowd," grinned Harrigan.

CHAPTER 10

THEY STARTED working eagerly to revive her. While McTee bathed her face and throat with handfuls of the sea water, Harrigan worked to liberate her from the twine. It was not easy. The twine was wet, and the knot held fast. Finally he gnawed it in two with his teeth. McTee, at the same time, elicited a faint moan. Her wrist was bruised and swollen rather than dangerously cut. Harrigan stuffed the twine into his hip pocket; then the two Adams carried their Eve to the shade of a tree and watched the color come back to her face by slow degrees.

The wind now increased suddenly as it had done on the evening of the wreck. It rose even as the day darkened, and in a moment it was rushing through the trees screaming in a constantly rising crescendo. The rain was coming, and against that tropical squall shelter was necessary.

The two men ran down the beach and returned dragging the ponderous section of the wheelhouse. They leaned the frame against two trunks at the same instant that the first big drops of rain rattled against it. Overhead they were quite securely protected by the dense and interweaving foliage of the two trees, but still the wind whistled in at either side and over and under the frame of boards. Of one accord they dropped beside their patient.

She was trembling violently; they heard the light, continuous chattering of her teeth. After her many hours under the merciless sun, this sudden change of temperature might bring on the fever against which they could not fight. They stripped off their shirts and wound them carefully around her shivering body. McTee lifted her in his arms and sat down with his back to the wind. Harrigan took a place beside him, and they caught her close. They seemed to be striving by the force of their will to drive the heat from their own blood into her trembling body. But still she moaned in her delirium, and the shivering would not stop.

Then the great idea came to Harrigan. He rose without a word and ran out into the rain to a fallen tree which must have been blown down years before, for now the trunk and the splintered stump were rotten to the core. He had noticed it that day. There was only a rim of firm wood left of the wreck. The stump gave readily enough under his pull. He ripped away long strips of the casing, bark and wood, and carried it back to the shelter. He made a second trip to secure a great armful of the powder-dry time-rotted core of the stump.

His third expedition carried him a little farther afield to a small sapling which he could barely make out through the night. He bent down the top of the little tree and snapped off about five feet of its length. This in turn he brought to the shelter. He stopped short here, frozen with amazement. The girl was raving in her delirium, and to soothe her, McTee was singing to her horrible sailor chanteys, pieced out with improvised and foolish words.

Harrigan listened only while his astonishment kept him helpless; then he took up his work. He first stripped away the twigs from his sapling top. Then he tied the twine firmly at either end of the stick, leaving the string loose. Next he fumbled among the mass of rubbish he had brought in from the rotten trunk and broke off a chunk of hard wood several inches in length. By rubbing this against the fragment of the wheelhouse, he managed to reduce one end of the little stick to a rough point.

He took the largest slab of the rim wood from the stump and knelt upon it to hold it firm. On this wood he rested his peg, which was wrapped in several folds of the twine and pressed down by the second fragment of wood. When he moved the long stick back and forth, the peg revolved at a tremendous rate of speed, its partially sharpened end digging into the wood on which it rested. It is a method of starting a fire which was once familiarly used by Indians.

For half an hour Harrigan sweated and groaned uselessly over his labor. Once he smelled a taint of smoke and shouted his triumph, but the peg slipped and the work was undone. He started all over again after a short rest and the peg creaked against the slab of wood with the speed of its rotation—a small sound of protest drowned by the bellowing of the storm and the ringing songs of McTee. Now the smoke rose again and this time the peg kept firm. The smoke grew pungent; there was a spark, then a glow, and it spread and widened among the powdery, rotten wood which Harrigan had heaped around his rotating peg.

He tossed the peg and bow aside and blew softly and steadily on the glowing point. It spread still more and now a small tongue of flame rose and flickered. Instantly Harrigan laid small bits of wood criss-cross on the pile of tinder. The flame licked at them tentatively, recoiled, rose again and caught hold. The fire was well started.

With gusts of wind fanning it roughly, the flame rose fast. Harrigan made other journeys to the rotten stump and wrenched away great chunks of bark and wood. He came back and piled them on the fire. It towered high, the upper tongues twisting among the branches of the tree. They laid Kate Malone between the windbreak and the fire. In a short time her trembling ceased; she turned her face to the blaze and slept.

They watched her with jealous care all night. In lieu of a pillow they heaped some of the wood dust from the stump beneath her head. When their large hands hovered over her to straighten the clothes which the wind fluttered, she seemed marvelously delicate and fragile. It was astonishing that so fragile a creature should have lived through the buffeting of the sea.

Toward morning the storm fell at a breath and the rain died away. They agreed that it might be safe to leave her alone while they ventured out to look for food, and at the first hint of light they started out, one to the north, and one to the south. Harrigan started at an easy run. He felt a joyous exultation like that of a boy eager for play. He tried to find shellfish first, but without success. His search carried him far down the beach to a group of big rocks rolling out to sea. On the leeward side of these rocks, in little hollows of the stone, he found a quantity of the eggs of some seafowl. They were quite large, the shells a dirty, faint blue and apparently very thick. He collected all he could carry and started back.

As he approached the shelter, he heard voices and stopped short with a sudden pang; McTee had returned first and awakened the girl. Harrigan sighed. He knew now how he had wanted to watch her eyes open for the first time, the cool sea-green eyes lighted by bewilderment, surprise, and joy. All that delight had been McTee's. It was that dark, handsome face she had seen leaning over her when she awoke. He was firmly implanted in her mind by this time as her savior. She opened her eyes, hungered, and she had seen McTee bringing food. Harrigan drew a long breath and went on slowly with lowered head.

They sat cross-legged, facing each other. The captain was showing Kate his prizes, which seemed to consist of a quantity of shellfish. She clapped her hands at something McTee said, and her laughter, wonderfully clear, reminded Harrigan of the chiming of faraway church bells. Blind anger suddenly possessed him as he stood by the fire glowering down at them.

CHAPTER 11

"EGGS! HOW perfectly wonderful, Mr. Harrigan! And I'm starved!"

She looked up to him, radiant with delight; but the triumphant eye of Harrigan fell not upon her but on McTee, who had suddenly grown pensive.

"But how can we cook them? There's nothing to boil water in—and no pan for frying them," ventured McTee.

"Roast 'em," said Harrigan scornfully. "Like this."

He wrapped several eggs in wet clay and placed them in the glowing ashes of the fire which had now burned low.

"While they're cooking," said McTee, "I'm going off. I've an idea."

Harrigan watched him with a shade of suspicion while he retreated. He turned his head to find Kate studying him gravely.

"Before you came, Mr. Harrigan—"

"My name's Dan. That'll save time."

"While you were gone," she went on, thanking him with a smile, "Captain McTee told me a great many things about you."

Harrigan stirred uneasily.

"Among other things, that you had no such record as he hinted at while we were on the *Mary Rogers*. So I have to ask you to forgive me—"

The blue eyes grew bright as he watched her.

"I've forgotten all that, for the sea washed it away from my mind."

"Really?"

"As clean as the wind has washed the sky."

Not a cloud stained the broad expanse from horizon to horizon.

"That's a beautiful way to put it. Now that we are here on the island, we begin all over again and forget what happened on the ship?"

"Aye, all of it."

"Shake on it."

He took her hand, but so gingerly that she laughed.

35

"We have to be careful of you," he explained seriously. "Here we are, as McTee puts it, on the rim of the world, two men an' one woman. If something happens to one of us, a third of our population's gone."

"A third of our population! Then I'm very important?"

"You are."

He was so serious that it disconcerted her. It suddenly became impossible for her to meet his eyes, they burned so bright, so eager, with something like a threat in them. She hailed the returning figure of McTee with relief.

He came bearing a large gourd, and he knelt before Kate so that she might look into it. She cried out at what she saw, for he had washed the inside of the gourd and filled it with cool water from the spring.

"Look!" said she to Harrigan. "It's water—and my throat is fairly burning."

"Humph," growled Harrigan, and he avoided the eye of McTee.

The gourd was too heavy and clumsy for her to handle. The captain had to raise and tip it so that she might drink, and as she drank, her eyes went up to his with gratitude.

Harrigan set his teeth and commenced raking the roasted eggs from the hot ashes. When her thirst was quenched, she looked in amazement at Harrigan; even his back showed anger. In some mysterious manner it was plain that she had displeased the big Irishman.

He turned now and offered her an egg, after removing the clay mold. But when she thanked him with the most flattering of smiles, she became aware that McTee in turn was vexed, while the Irishman seemed perfectly happy again.

"Have an egg, McTee," he offered, and rolled a couple toward the big captain.

"I will not. I never had a taste for eggs."

"Why, captain," murmured Kate, "you can't live on shellfish?"

"Humph! Can't I? Very nutritious, Kate, and very healthful. Have to be careful what you eat in this climate. Those eggs, for instance. Can you tell, Harrigan, whether or not they're fresh?"

Harrigan, his mouth full of egg, paused and glared at the captain.

"For the captain of a ship, McTee," he said coldly, "your head is packed with fool ideas. Eat your fish an' don't spoil the appetites of others."

He turned to Kate.

"These eggs are new-laid—they're—they're not more than twenty-four hours old."

His glance dared McTee to doubt the statement. The captain accepted the challenge.

"I suppose you watched 'em being laid, Harrigan?"

Harrigan sneered.

"I can tell by the taste partly and partly"—here he cracked the shell of another egg and, stripping it off, held up the little white oval to the light—"and partly by the color. It's dead white, isn't it?"

"Yes."

"That shows it's fresh. If there was a bit of blue in it, it'd be stale."

McTee breathed hard.

"You win," he said. "You ought to be on the stage, Harrigan."

But Harrigan was deep in another egg. Kate watched the two with covert glances, amazed, wondering. They had saved each other from death at sea, and now they were quarreling bitterly over the qualities of eggs.

And not eggs alone, for McTee, not to be outdone in courtesy, passed a handful of his shellfish to Harrigan. The Irishman regarded the fish and then McTee with cold disgust.

"D'you really think I'm crazy enough to eat one of these?" he queried.

Black McTee was black indeed as he glowered at the big Irishman.

"Open up; let's hear what you got to say about these shellfish," he demanded.

Harrigan announced laconically: "Scurvy."

"What?" This from Kate and McTee at one breath.

"Sure. There ain't any salt in 'em. No salt is as bad as too much salt. A friend of mine was once in a place where he couldn't get any salt food, an' he ate a lot of these shellfish. What was the result? Scurvy! He hasn't a tooth in his head today. An' he's only thirty."

"Why didn't you tell me?" cried Kate indignantly, and she laid a tentative finger against her white teeth, as if expecting to find them loose.

"I didn't want to hurt McTee's feelin's. Besides, maybe a few of them won't hurt you—much!"

McTee suddenly burst into laughter, but there was little mirth in the sound.

"Maybe you know these are the great blue clams that are famous for their salt."

"Really?" said Kate, greatly relieved.

"Yes," went on McTee, his eyes wandering slightly. "This species of clam has an unusual organ by which it extracts some of the salt from the sea water while taking its food. Look here!"

He held up a shell and indicated a blue-green spot on the inside.

"You see that color? That's what gives these clams their name and this is also the place where the salt deposit forms. This clam has a high percentage of salt—more than any other."

Harrigan, sending a bitter side glance at McTee, rose to bring some more wood, for it was imperative that they should keep the fire burning always.

"I'm so glad," said Kate, "that we have both the eggs and the clams to rely on. At least they will keep us from starving in this terrible place."

"H'm. I'm not so sure about the eggs."

He eyed them with a watering mouth, for his raging hunger had not been in the least appeased by the shellfish.

"But I'll try one just to keep you company."

He peeled away the shell and swallowed the egg hastily, lest Harrigan, returning, should see that he had changed his mind.

"Maybe the eggs are all right," he admitted as soon as he could speak, and he picked up another, "but between you and me, I'll confess that I shall not pay much attention to what Harrigan has to say. He's never been to sea before. You can't expect a landlubber to understand all the conditions of a life like this."

But a new thought which was gradually forming in her brain made Kate reserve judgment. Harrigan came back and placed a few more sticks of wood on the fire.

"I can't understand," said Kate, "how you could make a fire without a sign of a match."

"That's simple," said McTee easily. "When a man has traveled about as much as I have, he has to pick up all sorts of unusual ways of doing things. The way we made that fire was to—"

"The way *we* made it?" interjected Harrigan with bitter emphasis.

Kate frowned as she glanced from one to the other. There was the same deep hostility in their eyes which she had noticed when they faced each other in the captain's cabin aboard the *Mary Rogers*.

"An' why were ye sittin' prayin' for fire with the gir-rl thremblin' and freezin' to death in yer ar-rms if ye knew so well how to be makin' one?"

"Hush—Dan," said Kate; for the fire of anger blew high.

McTee started.

"You know each other pretty well, eh?"

"Tut, tut!" said Harrigan airily. "You can't expect a slip of a girl to be calling a black man like *you* by the front name?"

McTee moistened his white lips. He rose.

"I'm going for a walk—I always do after eating."

And he strode off down the beach. Harrigan instantly secured a handful of the shellfish.

"Speakin' of salt," he said apologetically, "I'll have to try a couple of these to be sure that the captain's right. I can tell by a taste or two."

He pried open one of the shells and ate the contents hastily, keeping one eye askance against the return of McTee.

"Maybe he's right about these shellfish," he pronounced judicially, "but it's a hard thing an' a dangerous thing to take the word of a man like McTee—he's that hasty. We must go easy on believin' what he says, Kate."

CHAPTER 12

THEN UNDERSTANDING flooded Kate's mind like waves of light in a dark room. She tilted back her head and laughed, laughed heartily, laughed till the tears brimmed her eyes. The gloomy scowl of Harrigan stopped her at last. As her mirth died out, the tall form of McTee appeared suddenly before them with his arms crossed. Where they touched his breast, the muscles spread out to a giant size. He was turned toward her, but the gleam of his eye fell full upon Harrigan.

"I suppose," said McTee, and his teeth clicked after each word like the bolt of a rifle shot home, "I suppose that you were laughing at me?"

The Irishman rose and faced the Scotchman, his head thrust forward and a devil in his eyes.

"An' what if we were, Misther McTee?" he purred. "An' what if we wer-r-re, I'm askin'?"

Kate leaped to her feet and sprang between them.

"Is there anything we can do," she broke in hurriedly, "to get away from the island?"

"A raft?" suggested Harrigan.

McTee smiled his contempt.

"A raft? And how would you cut down the trees to make it?"

"Burn 'em down with a circle of fire at the bottom."

"And then set green logs afloat? And how fasten 'em together, even supposing we could burn them down and drag them to the water? No, there's no way of getting off the island unless a boat passes and catches a glimpse of our fire."

"Then we'll have to move this fire to the top of the hill," said Harrigan.

"Suppose we go now and look over the hill and see what dry wood is near it," said McTee.

"Good."

Something in their eagerness had a meaning for Kate.

"Would you both leave me?" she reproached them.

"It was McTee suggested it," said Harrigan.

McTee favored his comrade with a glance that would have made any other man give ground. It merely made Harrigan grin.

"We'll draw straws for who goes and who stays," said McTee.

Kate picked up two bits of wood.

"The short one stays," she said.

"Draw," said Harrigan in a low voice.

"I was taught manners young," said McTee. "After you."

They exchanged glares again. The whole sense of her power over these giants came home to her as she watched them fighting their duel of the eyes.

"You suggested it," she said to McTee.

He stepped forward with an expression as grim as that of a prize fighter facing an antagonist of unknown prowess. Once and again his hand hovered above the sticks before he drew.

"You've chosen the walk to the hill," she said, and showed the shorter stick. "Do you mind?"

"No," mocked Harrigan, "he always walks after meals."

Their eyes dwelt almost fondly upon each other. They were both men after the other's heart. Then the Scotchman turned and strode away.

Kate watched Harrigan suspiciously, but his eyes, following McTee, were gentle and dreamy.

"Ah," he murmured, "there's a jewel of a man."

"Do you like him so much?"

"Do I like him? Me dear, I love the man; I'll break his head with more joy than a shtarvin' man cracks a nut!"

He recovered himself instantly.

"I didn't mean that—I—"

"Dan, you and McTee have planned to fight!"

He growled: "If a man told me that, I'd say he was a liar."

"Yes; but you won't lie to a girl, Harrigan."

She rose and faced him, reaching up to lay her hands on his thick shoulders.

"Will you give me your promise as an honest man to try to avoid a fight with him?"

For she saw death in it if they met alone; certainly death for one, and perhaps for both.

"Kate, would you ask a tree to promise to avoid the lightning?"

She caught a little breath through set teeth in her angry impatience, then: "Dan, you're like a naughty boy. Can't you be reasonable?"

Despite her wrath, she noticed a quick change in his face. The blue of his eyes was no longer cold and incurious, but lighted, warm, and marvelously deep.

And she said rapidly, making her voice cold to quell the uneasy, rising fire behind his eyes: "If you have made McTee angry, aren't you man enough to smooth things over—to ask his pardon?"

He answered vaguely: "Beg his pardon?"

"Why is that so impossible? For my sake, Dan!"

The light went out of his face as if a candle had been snuffed.

"For you, Kate?"

Then she understood her power fully for the first time, and found the thing which she must do.

"For me. I—I—"

She let her head droop, and then glanced up as if beseeching him to ask no questions.

"Look me square in the eye—so!"

He caught her beneath the chin with a grip that threatened a bruise, and his eyes burned down upon her.

"Are ye playin' with me, Kate? Are ye tryin' to torment me, or do ye really care for McTee?"

She tried with all her might, but could not answer. The rumble and ring of his voice brought her heart to her throat.

"You're tremblin'," said Harrigan, and he released her. "So it's all true. McTee!"

He turned on his heel like a soldier, lest she should mark the change of his expression; but she must have noticed something, for she called: "Harrigan—Dan!"

He stopped, but would not face her.

"You have your hands clenched. Are you going out to hunt for McTee in that black mood?"

"Kate," said Harrigan, "by my honor I'm swearin' he's as safe in my hands as a child."

CHAPTER 13

HARRIGAN STRODE off through the trees. To loosen the tight, aching muscles of his throat he began to sing—old Irish songs with a wail and a swing to them. He had taken no certain direction, for he only wished to be alone and far away from the other two; but after a time he realized that he was on the side of the central hill to which McTee had gone to look for the dry wood. Above all things in the world he wished to avoid the Scotchman now, and as soon as he became conscious of his whereabouts, he veered sharply to the right. He had scarcely walked a minute in the new direction before he met McTee. The latter had seen him first, and now stood with braced feet in his position of battle, rolling the sleeves of his shirt away from his forearms. Harrigan stepped behind a tree.

"Come out," roared McTee. "I've seen you. Don't try to sneak behind and take me from the back."

With an exceeding bitterness of heart, Harrigan stepped into view again.

"You look sick," went on McTee. "If you knew what would happen when we met, why did you come? If you fear me, go back and hug the skirts of the girl. She'll take pity on you, Harrigan."

The Irishman groaned. "Think your thoughts an' say your say, McTee. I can't lay a hand on you today."

The latter stepped close, stupefied with wonder.

"Do I hear you right? Are you taking water, Harrigan?"

Harrigan bowed his head, praying mutely for strength to endure.

"Don't say it!" pleaded McTee. "I've hunted the world and worn the roads bare looking for one man who could stand up to me—and now that I've found him, he turns yellow inside!"

And he looked upon the Irishman with a sick horror, as if the big fellow were turning into a reptile before his eyes. On the face of Harrigan there was an expression like that of the starving man whom the fear of poison induces to push away food.

"There's no word I can speak to you, McTee. You could never understand. Go back to the girl. Maybe she'll explain."

"The girl?"

At the wild hope in that voice Harrigan shuddered, and he could not look up.

"Harrigan, what do you mean?"

"Don't ask me. Leave me alone, McTee."

"Here's a mystery," said the Scotchman, "and our little party is postponed. The date is changed, that's all. Remember!"

He stepped off through the trees in the direction of the shelter on the beach, leaving Harrigan to throw himself upon the ground in a paroxysm of shame and hate.

But McTee, with hope to spur him on—a vague hope; a thought half formed and therefore doubly delightful—went with great strides until he came to Kate where she sat tending the fire. He broke at once into the heart of his question.

"I met Harrigan. He's changed. Something has happened. Tell me what it is. He says you know."

He crouched close to her, intent and eager, his eyes ready to read a thousand meanings into the very lowering of her lashes; but she let her glance rove past him.

"Well?" he asked impatiently.

"It is hard to speak of it."

Cold doubt fell upon the captain; he moistened his lips before he spoke.

"Hit straight from the shoulder. There's something between you and the Irishman?"

She dropped a hand over his mighty fist.

"After all, you are our only friend, Angus. Why shouldn't you know?"

He stood up and made a few paces to and fro, his hands locked behind him and his leonine head fallen low.

"Yes, why shouldn't you tell me! I think I understand already."

All desire to laugh went from her, and deep fear took its place; her eyes were held fascinated upon his interlaced fingers, white under their own terrific pressure; yet she understood that she must go on. If she failed, this mighty force would be turned against Harrigan; and Harrigan, not less grim in battle, as she could guess, would be turned against him.

She said quickly, to conceal her fear: "I thought there was some trouble between you and Dan. I asked him to promise that he would not fight with you. But I don't need to ask you to promise not to fight with him, for now that you know—"

He leaped up and beat his hands together over his head.

"And that was why! I taunted him and all the time he was laughing to himself!"

He stopped and then whispered to himself: "Still, it's only postponed. The tune will come! The time will come!"

She understood the promise.

"Angus! What are you saying?"

He said quietly: "Harrigan's safe from me while you care for him. Do you think I'm fool enough to make a martyr of him? Not I! But when we get back to the world—"

He finished the sentence by slowly flexing his fingers.

"I love you, Kate, and until the strength goes out of my hands, I'll still love you. I want you; and what I want I get. You'll hate me for it, eh?"

He went off without waiting for an answer, stumbling as he walked like one who was dazed. Her strength held with her until he was out of sight among the trees, but then she sank to the ground, panting. Sooner or later they were sure to discover her ruse, and the moment one of them learned that she did not love the other, they would rush into battle. She only prayed that the discovery would not come till they were safely off the island. Once back in the world the strong arm of the law might suffice to keep them apart.

The falling of the fire roused her at last and she set about gathering wood to keep it alive. It was the Irishman who returned first. He waved her to the shade of the shelter and finished collecting the wood.

CHAPTER 14

AFTERWARD HE inquired, frowning: "Where's McTee? I met him an' he started back to find you."

"He's gone off with his thoughts, Dan."

Harrigan sighed, looking up to the stainless blue of the sky: "Aye, that's the way of the Scotch. When they're happy in love, they go off by themselves an' brood like a dog that's thinking of a fight. But were I he, I'd never be leavin' your side, colleen."

His head tilted back in the way she had come to know, and she waited for the soft dialect: "I'd be singin' songs av love an' war-r-r, an' braggin' me hear-rt out, an' talkin' av the sea-green av your eyes, colleen. Look at him now!"

For the great form of McTee left the circle of the trees and approached them.

"He's got his head down between his shoulders like a whipped cur. He's broodin', an' his soul is thick in a fog."

"Dan, I trust you to cheer him up; but you'll not speak of me?"

"Not I. He's a proud man, Black McTee, an' he'd be angered to the core of him if he thought you'd talked about him an' his love to Harrigan. Whisht, Kate, I'll handle him like fire!

"The wood," he began, as McTee came in. "Did you find it on top of the hill, lad?"

McTee rumbled after a pause, and without looking at Harrigan: "There's plenty of it there. I made a little heap of the driest on the crown of the hill."

"Then the next thing is to move our fire up there."

"Move our fire?" cried Kate. "How can you carry the fire?"

"Easy. Take two pieces of burnin' wood an' walk along holdin' them close together. That way they burn each other an' the flame keeps goin'. Watch!"

He selected two good-sized brands from the fire and raised them, holding one in either hand and keeping the ignited portions of the sticks together. McTee looked from Kate to Harrigan.

"Sit down and talk to Kate. I'll carry the sticks; I know where the pile of timber is."

Harrigan made a significant and covert nod and winked at McTee with infinite understanding.

"Stay here yourself, lad. I wouldn't be robbing you——"

Kate coughed for warning, and he broke off sharply.

"You've made one trip to the hill. This is my turn. Besides, you wouldn't know how to keep the stick burnin'. I've done it before."

McTee stared, agape with astonishment. The meaning of that wink still puzzled his brain. He turned to Kate for explanation, and she beckoned him to stay. When Harrigan disappeared, he said: "What's the meaning? Doesn't Harrigan want to be with you?"

She allowed her eyes to wander dreamily after Harrigan.

"Don't you see? He's like a big boy. He's overflowing with happiness and he has to go off to play by himself."

McTee watched her with deep suspicion.

"It's queer," he pondered. "I know the Irish like a book, and when they're in love, they're always singing and shouting and raising the devil. It looked to me as if Harrigan was making himself be cheerful."

He went on: "I'll take him aside and tell him that I understand. Otherwise he'll think he's fooling me."

"Please! You won't do that? Angus, you know how proud he is! He will be furious if he finds out that I've spoken to you about—about—our love. Won't you wait until he tells you of his own accord?"

He ground his teeth in an ugly fury.

"You understand? If I find you've been playing with me, it'll mean death for Harrigan, and worse than that for you?"

She made her glance sad and gentle.

"Will you never trust me, Angus?"

He answered, with a sort of wonder at himself: "Since I was a child, you are the first person in the world who has had the right to call me by my first name."

"Not a single woman?" and she shivered.

"Not one."

She pondered: "No love, no friendship, not even pity to bring you close to a single human being all your life?"

"No child has ever come near me, for I've never had room for pity. No man has been my friend, for I've spent my time fighting them and breaking them. And I've despised women too much to love them."

The tears rose to her eyes as she spoke: "I pity you from the bottom of my soul!"

"Pity? Me? By God, Kate, you'll teach me to hate you!"

"I can't help it. Why, if you have never loved, you have never lived!"

"You talk like a girl in a Sunday school! Ha, have I never lived? Men were made strong so that a stronger man should be their master; and women—"

"And women, Angus?"

"All women are fools; one woman is divine!"

The yearning of his eyes gave a bitter meaning to his words, and she was shaken like a leaf blown here and there by contrary winds. Unheeded, the sudden tropic night swooped upon them like the shadow of a giant bird, and as the dark increased, they saw the glimmering of the fire upon the hill. She rose, and he followed her until they reached the upward slope.

Then he said: "You will want to be alone with him for a time. Can you find the rest of the way?"

"Yes. You'll come soon?"

"I'll come soon, but I have to be by myself for a while. I may hate you for it afterward, but now I'm weak and soft inside—like a child—and I only wish for your happiness."

"God bless you, Angus!"

"God help me," he answered harshly, and stepped into the blank night of the shadow of the trees.

Harrigan shook his head in wonder when he saw her coming alone. He had built up the fire and heaped fresh fuel in towering piles nearby. The flames shot up twenty and thirty feet, making a wide signal across the sea.

"He's gone off by himself again?" questioned the Irishman.

She complained: "I can't understand him. Will he be always like this? What shall I do, Dan?"

He met her appeal with a smile, but the blue eyes went cold at once and he sighed. It would never do to have the two sitting silent beside that fire. The brooding of McTee would excite no suspicions in the mind of Harrigan, but the quiet of the Irishman would be sure to excite the suspicions of the other.

"Will you do something for me, Dan?"

He looked up with a whimsical yearning.

"Teach McTee manners? Aye, with all me heart!"

She laughed: "No; but cheer him up. You said that if you were in his place, you'd be singing all the time."

"And I would."

"Then sing for me—for Angus and me—tonight when we're sitting by the fire. He's fallen into a brooding melancholy, and I can't altogether trust him. Can you understand?"

"And I'm to do the cheering up?"

"You won't fail me?"

He turned and occupied himself for a moment by hurling great armfuls of wood upon the fire. The flames burst up with showering sparks, roaring and leaping. Then, as if inspired by the sight, he came to her with his head tilting back hi the way he had.

"I'll do it—I'll sing my heart out for you."

As McTee came up, the three sat down; a strange group, for the two men stared fixedly before them at the fire, conscientiously avoiding any movement of the eyes toward Kate and the other; and she sat between them, watching each of them covertly and humming all the while as if from happiness. Each of them thought the humming a love song meant for the ears of the other. Finally McTee turned and stared curiously, first at Kate and then at Harrigan. Manifestly he could not understand either their silence or their aloofness. It was for the Scotchman that she would have to play her role; Harrigan was blind. The Irishman also, as if he felt the eyes of McTee, turned his head. Kate nodded significantly and moved closer to him.

Obedient to his promise, he turned away again and raised his head to sing. Alternate light and shadow swept across his face and made fire and dark in his hair as the wind tossed the flame back and forth. At the other side of her McTee rested upon one elbow. Whenever she turned her head, she caught the steel-cold glitter of his eyes.

The first note from Harrigan's lips was low and faltering and off key; she trembled lest McTee should understand, but the Scotchman attributed the emotion to another cause. As his singing continued, moreover, it increased hi power and steadiness. One thing, however, she had not counted on, and that was the emotion of Harrigan. Every one of his songs carried on the theme of love in a greater or less degree, and now his own singing swept him beyond the bounds of caution; he turned directly to Kate and sang for her alone "Kathleen Mavourneen." There was love and farewell at once in his singing, there was yearning and despair.

She knew that a crisis had come, and that McTee was pressed to the limits of his endurance. The game had gone too far, and yet she dared not appear indifferent to the singing. That would have been too direct a betrayal, so she sat with her head back and a smile on her lips.

There was a groan and a stifled curse. McTee rose; the song died in the throat of Harrigan.

CHAPTER 15

"IS THIS what you feared?" said the Scotchman. "Is this what you wanted protection against? No; you're in league together to torture me, and all this time you've been laughing up your sleeves at my expense!"

"At your expense?" growled Harrigan, rising in turn. "Is it at your expense that I've been sittin' here breakin' me heart with singin' love tunes for you an' the girl?"

She sprang up in an agony of fear.

"Go! Go!" she begged of McTee. "If you doubt me, go, and when you come back calm, I will explain."

He brushed her to one side and made a step toward Harrigan.

"Love songs for *me?*" he repeated incredulously.

"Aye, love songs for you. Ye black swine, ye could not be happy till I was brought in to be the piper while you an' Kate danced!"

"While I and Kate danced?" thundered McTee. "My God, man—"

He broke off short, and a cruel light of understanding was in his eyes.

"Harrigan," he said quietly, "did Kate tell you she loved me?"

"Ye fool! Why else am I sittin' here singin' for your sake? Would I not rather be amusin' myself by takin' the hollow of your throat under my thumbs—so?"

McTee laughed softly, and Kate could not meet his eye.

"Well?" he said.

"Yes, I lied to you."

She turned to Harrigan: "And to you. Don't you see? I found you on the verge of a fight, and I knew that in it you would both be killed. What else could I do? I hoped that for my sake you would spare each other. Was it wrong of me, Dan? Angus, will you forgive me?"

Harrigan raised his arms high above his head and stretched like one from whose wrists the manacles have been unlocked after a long imprisonment.

"McTee, are ye ready? There's a weight gone off my soul!"

"Harrigan, I've been a driver of men, but this girl has put me under the whip. When I'm through with you, I'm coming back to her."

"It'll be your ghost that returns."

Kate hesitated one instant as if to judge which was the greatest force toward evil. Then she dropped to her knees and caught the hands of McTee, those strong, cruel hands.

"If you will not fight, I'll—I'll be kind to you, I'll be everything you ask of me—"

"You're pleading for him?"

"No, no! For him and for you; for your two souls!"

"Bah! Mine was lost long ago, and I'll answer that there's a claim on Harrigan filed away in hell. He's too strong to have lived clean."

"Angus, we're all alone here—on the rim of the world, you've said—and in places like this the eye of God is on you."

He laughed brutally: "If He sees me, He'll look the other way."

"Have done with the chatter," broke in Harrigan. "Ah-h, McTee, I see where my hands'll fit on your throat."

"Come," McTee answered without raising his voice; "there's a corner of the beach where a current stands in close by the shore. You've been a traveling man, Harrigan. When I've killed you, I'll throw your body into the sea, and the tide will take you out to see the rest of the world."

"Come," said Harrigan; "I'd as soon finish you there as here, and when you're dead, I'll sit you up against a tree and come down every day to watch you rot."

The girl fell to the ground between them with her face buried in her arms, silent. The two men lowered their eyes for a moment upon her, and then turned and walked down the hill, going shoulder to shoulder like friends. So they came out upon the beach and walked along it until they reached the point of which McTee had spoken.

It was a level, hard-packed stretch of sand which offered firm footing and no rocks over which one of the fighters might stumble at a critical moment.

"'Tis a lovely spot," sighed Harrigan. "Captain, you're a jewel of a man to have thought of it."

"Aye, this is no deck at sea that can heave and twist and spoil my work."

"It is not; and the palms of my hands are almost healed. Had you thought of that, captain?"

"As you lie choking, Harrigan, think of the girl. The minute I've heaved you into the sea, I go back to her."

The hard breathing of the Irishman filled up the interval.

"I see one thing clear. It's that I'll have to kill you slow. A man like you, McTee, ought to taste his death a while before it comes. Come to me ar-rms, captain, I've a little secret to whisper in your ear. Whisht! 'Twill not be long in the tellin'!"

McTee replied with a snarl, and the two commenced to circle slowly, drawing nearer at every step. On the very edge of leaping forward, Harrigan was astonished to see McTee straighten from his crouch and point out to sea.

"The eye of God!" muttered the Scotchman. "She was right!"

Harrigan jumped back lest this should prove a maneuver to place him off his guard, and then looked in the indicated direction. It was true; a point of light, a white eye, peered at them from far across the water. Then the shout of McTee rang joyously: "A ship!"

"The fire!" answered Harrigan, and pointed back to the hill, for Kate had allowed the flames to fall in their absence.

All thought of the battle left them. They started back on the run to build high their signal light, and when they came to the top of the hill, they found Kate lying as they had left her. She started to her knees at the sound of their footsteps and stretched out her arms to them.

"God has sent you back to me!"

"A ship!" thundered McTee for answer, and he flung a great armful of wood upon the blaze. It rose with a rush, leaping and crackling, but all three kept at their work until the pile of wood was higher than their heads. Only when the supply of dry fuel was exhausted did they pause to look out to sea. In place of the one eye of white there were three lights, one of white, one of red, and one of green—the lights of a ship running in toward land.

In a moment the moon slipped up above the eastern waters, and right across that broad white circle moved a ship with the smoke streaming back from her funnel. Unquestionably the captain had seen the signal fire and understood its meaning.

They waited until the red light became fairly stationary, showing that the steamer had been laid-to. Then they ran for the beach and took up their position on the line between the glow of their fire and the position of the ship, guessing that in this way they would be on the spot where the ship's boat would be most likely to touch the shore.

"McTee," said Harrigan, "it may be half an hour before that boat reaches the beach. Is there any reason why both of us should go aboard it?"

"Harrigan, there is none! Stand up to me."

"If you do this," broke in Kate, "I will bring the sailors who come ashore to the spot where the dead man lies, and I'll tell how he died."

They looked at her, knowing that she could be trusted to fulfill that threat. The moon lay on the beauty of her face; never had she seemed so desirable. They looked to each other, and each seemed doubly hateful to the other.

"Kate, dear," said Harrigan hastily, "I see the boat come tossin' there over the water. Speak out like a brave girl. Neither of us will leave the other in peace as long as we have a hope of you. Choose between us before we put a foot in that boat, and if you choose McTee, I'll give you God's blessin' an' say no more nor ever raise my hand against ye. McTee, will ye do the like?"

"For the sake of the day of the fight and the wreck I will. If she chooses you now, I'll raise no hand against you."

A shout came faintly across the rush and ripple of the breakers.

"Speak out," said Harrigan.

"Hallo!" she screamed in answer to the hail from the boat, and then turning to them: "I choose neither of you!"

"McTee," growled Harrigan, "I'm thinkin' we've both been fools."

"Think what you will, I'll have her; and if you cross me again, I'll finish you, Harrigan."

"McTee, ten of your like couldn't finish me. But look! There's the girl wadin' out to the boat. Let's steady her through the waves."

They ran out and, catching her beneath the shoulders, bore her safe and high through the small rollers. When they were waist-deep, the boat swung near. A lantern was raised by the man in the bows, and under that light they saw the four men at the oars, now backing water to keep their boat from washing to the beach. The sailors cheered as the two men swung Kate over the gunwale and then clambered in after her. The man at the bows all this time had kept his lantern high above his head with a rigid arm, and now he bellowed: "Black McTee!"

"Right!" said McTee. "And you?"

"Salvain—put back for the ship, lads—Pietro Salvain. D'you mean to say you've forgotten me?"

"Shanghai!" said McTee, as light broke on his memory. "What a night that was."

"But you—"

"The *Mary Rogers* took a header for Davy Jones's locker; first mate drunk and ran her on a reef; all hands went under except the three of us; we drifted to this island."

"Black McTee shipwrecked! By God, if we get to port with our old tramp, I'll get a farm and stick to dry land."

"Your ship?"

"The *Heron* , four thousand tons, White Henshaw, skipper."

"White Henshaw?" cried McTee in almost reverent tones.

"The same. Old White still sticks to his wheel. He's as hard a man as you, McTee, in his own way."

They were pulling close to the freighter by this time, and Salvain gave quick orders to lay the boat alongside. In another moment they stood on the deck, where a tall man in white clothes advanced to meet them.

"Good fishing, sir," said Salvain. "We've picked up three shipwrecked people, with Angus McTee among them."

"Black McTee!" cried the other, and even in the dim light he picked out the towering form of the Scotchman.

"It took a wreck to bring us together, Captain Henshaw," said McTee, "but here we are, I've combed the South Seas for ten years for the sake of meeting you."

"H-m!" grunted Henshaw. "We'll drink on the strength of that. Come into the cabin."

They trooped after him, Salvain and the three rescued, and stood in the roomy cabin, the captain and the first mate dapper and cool in their white uniforms, the other three marvelously ragged. Barefooted, their hair falling in jags across their foreheads, their muscles bulging through the rents in their shirts, McTee and Harrigan looked battered but triumphant. Kate Malone might have been the prize which they had safely carried away. She was even more ragged than her companions, and now she withdrew into a shadowy corner of the cabin and shook the long, loose masses of her hair about her shoulders.

CHAPTER 16

THE DARK eye of Pietro Salvain was quick to note her condition. He was a rather small, lean-faced man with the skin drawn so tightly across his high cheekbones that it glistened. He was emaciated; his energy consumed him as hunger consumes other men.

"There is a berth for me below," he said to Kate. "You must take my room. And I have a cap, some silk shirts, a loose coat which you might wear—so?"

"This is Miss Malone, Salvain," said McTee before she could answer.

"You are very kind, Mr. Salvain," she said.

He smiled and bowed very low, and then opened the door for her; but all the while his glance was upon McTee, who stared at him so significantly that before following Kate through the door, Salvain shrugged his shoulders and made a gesture of resignation.

The captain turned to Harrigan. Henshaw was very old. He was always so erect and carried his chin so high that the loose skin of his throat hung in two sharp ridges. In spite of the tight-lipped mouth, the beaklike nose, and the small, gleaming eyes, there was something about his face which intensified his age. Perhaps it was the yellow skin, dry as the parchment from an Egyptian tomb and criss-crossed by a myriad little wrinkles.

"And you, sir?" he said to the Irishman.

"One of my crew," broke in McTee carelessly. "He'll be quite contented in the forecastle. Eh, Harrigan?"

"Quite," said Harrigan, and his glance acknowledged the state of war.

"Then if you'll go forward, Harrigan," said the captain, and his voice was dry and dead as his skin—"if you'll go forward and report to the bos'n, he'll see that you have a bunk."

"Thank you, sir," murmured Harrigan, and slipped from the room on his bare feet.

"That man," stated Henshaw, "is as strong as you are, McTee, and yet they call you the huskiest sailor of the South Seas."

"He is almost as strong," answered McTee with a certain emphasis.

Something like a smile appeared in the eyes of Henshaw, but did not disturb the fixed lines of his mouth. For a moment Henshaw and McTee measured each other.

The Scotchman spoke first: "Captain, you're as keen as the stories they tell of you."

"And you're as hard, McTee."

The latter waved the somewhat dubious compliment away.

"I was breaking that fellow, and he held out longer than any man I've ever handled. The shipwreck interrupted me, or I would have finished what I started."

"You'd like to have me finish what you began?"

"You read my mind."

"Discipline is a great thing."

"Absolutely necessary at sea."

Henshaw answered coldly: "There's no need for us to act the hypocrite, eh?"

McTee hesitated, and then grinned: "Not a bit. I know what you did twenty years ago in the Solomons."

"And I know the story of you and the pearl divers."

"That's enough."

"Quite."

"And Harrigan?"

"As a favor to you, McTee, I'll break him. Maybe you'll be interested in my methods."

"Try mine first. I made him scrub down the bridge with suds every morning, and while his hands were puffed and soft, I sent him down to the fireroom to pass coal."

"He'll kill you someday."

"If he can."

They smiled strangely at each other.

A knock came at the door, and Salvain entered, radiant.

"She is divine!" he cried. "Her hair is old copper with golden lights. McTee, if she is yours, you have found another Venus!"

"If she is not mine," answered McTee, "at least she belongs to no other man."

Salvain studied him, first with eagerness, then with doubt, and last of all with despair.

"If any other man said that I would question it—so!—with my life. But McTee? No, I love life too well!"

"Now," Henshaw said to Salvain, "Captain McTee and I have business to talk."

"Aye, sir," said Salvain.

"One minute, Salvain," broke in McTee. "I haven't thanked you in the girl's name for taking care of Miss Malone."

The first mate paused at the door.

"I begin to wonder, captain," he answered, "whether or not you have the right to thank me in her name!"

He disappeared through the door without waiting for an answer.

"Salvain has forgotten me," muttered McTee, balling his fist, "but I'll freshen his memory."

He flushed as he became aware of the cold eye of Henshaw upon him.

"Even Samson fell," said the old man. "But she hasn't cut your hair yet, McTee?"

"What the devil do you mean?"

Henshaw silently poured another drink and passed it to the Scotchman. The latter gripped the glass hard and tossed off the drink with a single gesture. At once his eyes came back to Henshaw's face with the fierce question. He was astonished to note kindliness in the answering gaze.

Old Henshaw said gently: "Tut, tut! You're a proper man, McTee, and a proper man has always the thought of some woman tucked away in his heart. Look at me! For almost sixty years I've been the King of the South Seas!"

At the thought of his glories his face altered, as soldiers change when they receive the order to charge.

"You're a rare man and a bold man, McTee, but you'll never be what White Henshaw has been—the Shark of the Sea! Ha! Yet think of it! Ten years ago, after all my harvesting of the sea, I had not a dollar to show for it! Why? Because I was working for no woman. But here I am sailing home from my last voyage—rich! And why? Because for ten years I've been working for a woman. For ourselves we make and we spend. But for a woman we make and we save. Aye!"

"For a woman?" repeated McTee, wondering. "Do you mean to say—"

"Tut, man, it's my granddaughter. Look!"

Perhaps the whisky had loosened the old man's tongue; perhaps these confidences were merely a tribute to the name and fame of McTee; but whatever was the reason, McTee knew he was hearing things which had never been spoken before. Now Henshaw produced a leather wallet from which he selected two pictures, and handed one to the Scotchman. It showed a little girl of some ten years with her hair braided down her back. McTee looked his question.

"That picture was sent to me by my son ten years ago."

It showed the effect of time and rough usage. The edges of the cheap portrait were yellow and cracked.

"He was worthless, that son of mine. So I shut him out of my mind until I got a letter saying he was about to die and giving his daughter into my hands. That picture was in the letter. Ah, McTee, how I pored over it! For, you see, I saw the face of my wife in the face of the little girl, Beatrice. She had come back to life in the second generation. I suppose that happens sometimes.

"I made up my mind that night to make a fortune for little Beatrice. First I sold my name and honor to get a half share and captaincy of a small tramp freighter. Then I went to the Solomon Islands. You know what I did there? Yes, the South Seas rang with it. It was brutal, but it brought me money.

"I sent enough of that money to the States to keep the girl in luxury. The rest of it I put back into my trading ventures. I got a larger boat. I did unheard-of things; and everything I touched turned into gold. All into gold!

"From time to time I got letters from Beatrice. First they were careful scrawls which said nothing. Then the handwriting grew more fluent. It alarmed me to notice the growth of her mind; I was afraid that when I finally saw her, she would see in me only a barbarian. So I educated myself in odd hours. I've read a book while a hurricane was standing my ship on her beam ends."

McTee, leaning forward with a frown of almost painful interest, understood. He saw it in the wild light of the old man's eyes; a species of insanity, this love of the old man for the child he had never seen.

"Notice my language now? Never a taint of the beach lingo in it. I rubbed all that out. Aye, McTee, it took me ten years to educate myself for that girl's sake. In the meantime, I made money, as I've said. Ten years of that!

"Beatrice was in college, and six months ago I got the word that she had graduated. A month later I heard that she was going into a decline. It was nothing very serious, but the doctors feared for the strength of her lungs. It made me glad. Now I knew that she would need me. An old man is like a woman, McTee; he needs to have things dependent on him.

"I turned everything I had into cash. I did it so hurriedly that I must have lost close to twenty per cent on the forced sales. What did I care? I had enough, and I made myself into a grandfather who could meet Beatrice's educated friends on their own level.

"I kept this old ship, the *Heron* , out of the list of my boats. I am going back to Beatrice with gold in my hands and gold in my brain! All for her. But is she not worth it? Look!"

He thrust the second portrait into McTee's hands. It showed a rather thin-faced girl with abnormally large eyes and a rather pathetic smile. It was an appealing face rather than a pretty one.

"Beautiful!" said McTee with forced enthusiasm.

"Yes, beautiful! A little pinched, perhaps, but she'll fill out as she grows older. And those are her grandmother's eyes! Aye!"

He took the photograph and touched it lightly.

His voice grew lower, and the roughness was plainly a tremolo now: "The doctors say she's sick, a little sick, quite sick, in fact. Twice every day I make them send me wireless reports of her condition. One day it's better—one day it's worse."

He began to walk the cabin, his step marvelously elastic and nervous for so aged a man.

"Is it not well, McTee? Let her be at death's door! I shall come to her bedside with gold in either hand and raise her up to life! She shall owe everything to me! Will that not make her love me? Will it?"

He grasped McTee's shoulder tightly.

"I'm not a pretty lad to look at, eh, lad?"

McTee poured himself a drink hastily, and drained the glass before he answered.

"A pretty man? Nonsense, Henshaw! A little weather-beaten, but a tight craft at that; she'll worship the ground you walk! Character, Henshaw, that's what these new American girls want to see in a man!"

Henshaw sighed with deep relief.

"Ah-h, McTee, you comfort me more than a drink on a stormy night! For reward, you shall see what I'm bringing back to her. Come!"

He rose and led McTee into his bedroom, for two cabins were retained for the captain's use. Filling one corner of the room was a huge safe almost as tall as a man.

He squatted before the safe and commenced to work the combination with a swift sureness which told McTee at once that the old buccaneer came here many times a day to gloat over his treasure. At length the door of the safe fell open. Inside was a great mass of little canvas bags. McTee was panting as if he had run a great distance at full speed.

"Take one."

The Scotchman raised one of the bags and shook it. A musical clinking sounded.

"Forty pounds of gold coin," said Henshaw, "and about ten thousand dollars in all. There are eighty-five of those bags, and every one holds the same amount. Also—"

He opened a little drawer at the top of the safe and took from it a chamois bag. When he untied it, McTee looked within and saw a quantity of pearls. He took out a small handful. They were chosen jewels, flawless, glowing. His hand seemed to overflow with white fire. He dropped them back in the bag, letting each pearl run over the end of his fingers. Henshaw restored the bag and locked the safe. Then the two men stared at each other. They had been opposite types the moment before, but now their lips parted in the same thirsty eagerness.

"If she were dead," said McTee almost reverently, "the sight of that would bring her back to life."

"McTee, you're a worthy lad. They've told me lies about you. Indeed it would bring her back to life! It must be so! And yet—" Sudden melancholy fell on him as they returned to the other room and sat down. "Yet I think night and day of what an old devil of a black magician told me in the Solomon Islands. He said I and my gold should burn together. I laughed at him and told him I could not die on dry land. He said I would not, but that I should burn at sea! Think of that, McTee! Suppose I should be robbed of the sight of my girl and of my gold at the same time!"

McTee started to say something cheerful, but his voice died away to a mutter. Henshaw was staring at the wall with visionary eyes filled with horror and despair.

"Lad, do you think ghosts have power?"

"Henshaw, you've drunk a bit too much!"

"If they have no power, I'm safe. I fear no living man!" He added softly: "No man but myself!"

"I'm tired out," said McTee suddenly. "Where shall I bunk, captain?"

"Here! Here in this room! Take that couch in the corner over there. It has a good set of springs. With gold in my hands. Here are some blankets. With gold in my hands and my brain. Though you don't need much covering in this latitude. I would raise her from the grave."

He went about, interspersing his remarks to McTee with half-audible murmurs addressed to his own ears.

"Is this," thought McTee, "the Shark of the South Seas?"

A knock came and the door opened. A fat sailor in an oilskin hat stood at the entrance.

"The cook ain't put out no lunch for the night watches, sir," he whined.

Henshaw had stood with his back turned as the door opened. He turned now slowly toward the open door. McTee could not see his face nor guess at its expression, but the moment the big sailor caught a glimpse of his skipper's countenance, he blanched and jumped back into the night, slamming the door behind him. That sight recalled something to McTee.

"One thing more, captain," he said. "What of Harrigan? Do we break him between us?"

"Aye, in your own way!"

"Good! Then start him scrubbing the bridge and send him down to the fireroom afterwards, eh?"

"It's done. Why do you hate him, McTee? Is it the girl?"

"No; the color of his hair. Good night."

CHAPTER 17

LONG BEFORE this, Harrigan had reported to the bos'n, burly Jerry Hovey, and had been assigned to a bunk into which he fairly dived and fell asleep in the posture in which he landed. In the morning he tumbled out with the other men and became the object of a crossfire of questions from the curious sailors who wanted to know all the details of the wreck of the *Mary Rogers* and the life on the island. He was saved from answering nine-tenths of the chatter by a signal from the bos'n, who beckoned Harrigan to a stool a little apart from the rest of the crew. Jerry Hovey was a cheery fellow of considerable bulk, with an habitual smile. That smile went out, however, when he talked with Harrigan, and the Irishman became conscious of a pair of steady, alert gray eyes.

"Look here," said Hovey, and he talked out of the corner of his mouth with a skill which would have become an old convict of many terms, "I've had it put to me straight that you're a hard one. Is that the right dope?"

Harrigan smiled.

"Because if it is," said Hovey, "we're the best gang at bustin' up these hard guys that ever walked the deck of a ship. If you try any side steps and fancy ducking of your work, there'll be a disciplinin' comin' your way at a gallop. Are you wise?"

Harrigan still smiled, but the coldness of his eye made the bos'n thoughtful. He was not one, however, to be easily cowed. Now he balled his fist and smote it against the palm of his other hand with a slap that resounded.

"On my own hook," he stated, "I can sling my mitts with the best of them, an' I'm always lookin' for work in that line. Now I'm sayin' all this in private, sonny, to let you know that Black McTee has wised up the skipper about you, and I'm keepin' a weather eye open. If you make one funny move, I'll be on your back."

"All right, Jerry."

"Don't call me Jerry, you swab! I'm the bos'n."

"Look me in the eye, Jerry Hovey, me dear. If you so much as bat the lashes av wan eye in lookin' at me, I'll bust ye in two pieces like a sea biscuit, Jerry, an' I'll eat the biggest half an' throw the rest into the sea. Ar-r-re ye wise?"

Now, Jerry Hovey was a very big man, and he had thrashed men of larger bulk than Harrigan. But there was something about the Irishman's thickness of shoulder and length of arm that gave him pause. So first of all Jerry grew very thoughtful indeed, and then his habitual smile returned. Nevertheless, Harrigan did not forget those gray, alert eyes.

The bos'n went on in a gentler voice: "I was tryin' you out, Harrigan. I'll lay to it that the cap'n has the wrong idea about you. But will you tell me why he's ridin' you?"

"Sure. It's Black McTee. Before the *Mary Rogers* went down, McTee was tryin' to break me. I guess he's asked this White Henshaw to try a hand. What have they got lined up for me?"

"You're to scrub down the bridge an' while your hands are still soft you go down to the fireroom an' pass coal. It'll tear your hands off, that work."

Harrigan was gray, but he answered. "That's an old story. McTee worked me like that all the time."

"An' you didn't break?" gasped Hovey.

Harrigan grinned, but his smile stopped when he noticed a certain calculation in the face of the bos'n.

"Mate," said Hovey, "I guess you're about ripe for something I'm goin' to say to you one of these days. Now go up to the bridge an' scrub it down."

With the prospect of the long torture before him once more, Harrigan in a daze picked up the bucket of suds to which he was pointed and went with his brush toward the bridge. Through the mist which enveloped his brain broke wild thoughts—to steal upon McTee at the first meeting and hurl his hated body overboard. Yet even in his bewildered condition he realized what such an act would mean. Murder on land is bad enough, but murder at sea is doubly damned by the law. It was in the power of White Henshaw to hang him up to the mast.

Revolving these dismal prospects with downward head, he climbed from the waist of the ship to the cabin promenade, and there a voice hailed him, and he turned to see Kate Malone approaching. She was all in white—cap, canvas shoes, silk shirt absurdly lose at the throat, and linen coat with the sleeves turned far back so that her hands would not be enveloped. The duck trousers were also taken up several reefs.

"Good morning," she said, and held out her hand.

He watched her smile wistfully, and then made a little gesture with his own hands, one burdened with the scrubbing brush and the other with the bucket.

"What does it mean?"

"Hell," said Harrigan.

"Explain."

"It's McTee again, damn his eyes!"

"Do you mean to say they've started to treat you as they did on the *Mary Rogers*? The scrubbing and then the work in the fireroom?"

"Right."

She stamped her foot in impotent fury.

"What manner of man is he, Dan? He's not all brute; why does he treat you like this?"

The Irishman smiled.

She cried with increasing anger: "What can I do?"

"Make your skin yellow an' your hair gray an' walk with no spring in your step. He wants to break me now because of you."

There was moist pity in her eyes, yet they gleamed with excitement at the thought of this battle of the Titans for her sake.

"I will go to him," she said after a moment, "and tell him that you mean nothing to me. Then he will stop."

The cold, incurious eyes studied her without passion, and once more he smiled.

"He'll not stop. Whether you like me or not, Kate, doesn't count. One of us'll go down, an' you'll be for the one that's left. He knows it—I know it."

"Harrigan!" called the voice of McTee from the bridge, and the tall Scotchman lifted his cap to Kate.

"I'm the slave," said Harrigan, "and there's the whip. Good-by."

She stamped her foot with an almost childish fury, saying: "Someday he shall regret this brutal tyranny. Good-by, Dan, and good luck!"

She took his hand in both of hers, but her eyes held spitefully upon the bridge, as if she hoped that McTee would witness the handshake; the captain, however, had turned his back upon them.

Dan muttered to himself as he climbed the bridge: "Did she do that to anger McTee or to please me?" And the thought so occupied his mind that he paid no attention to the Scotchman when he reached the bridge. He merely dropped to his knees and commenced scrubbing. McTee, in the meanwhile, loitered about the bridge as if on his own ship. In due time Harrigan drew near, the suds swishing under his brush. The Irishman, remembering suddenly, commenced to hum a tune.

"The old grind, eh, Harrigan?" said McTee.

The Irishman, humming idly still, looked up, calmly surveyed the captain, and then went on as if he had heard merely empty wind instead of words.

"After the scrubbing brush the shovel," went on McTee, but still Harrigan paid no attention. He rose when his task was completed and made his eyes gentle as if with pity while he gazed upon McTee.

"I'm sorry for you, McTee; you've made a hard fight; it's strange you've got no ghost of a chance of winnin'."

"What d'you mean?"

"Couldn't you hear her when she talked to me?"

"I could not."

"Couldn't you see her face? It was written there as plain as print."

McTee cleared his throat.

"What was written there?"

"The thing you want to see. When she took my hand in both of hers—"

"Hell!"

"Ah-h, man, it was wonderful! The scrubbing brush an' the shovel—they mean nothin' to me now."

"Harrigan, you're lying."

The latter dropped his scrubbing brush into the bucket of suds and stood with arms akimbo studying the captain.

"For a smart man, McTee, you've been a fool. I could of gone down on me knees an' begged to do what you've done. Don't you see? You've thrown her with her will or against it into me arms. I'm poor Harrigan, brave and downtrodden; you're Black McTee once more, the tyrant. She looks sick at the mention of your name."

"I never dreamed you'd go whining to her. I thought you were a man; you're only a spineless dog, Harrigan!"

"Am I that? She pities me, McTee, an' from pity it's only one step to something bigger. Can you trust me to lead her that one step? You can!"

"If I went to her and told her how you boasted of having won her?"

"She wouldn't believe what you said about me if you swore it with both hands on the Bible. Be wise, McTee. Give up the game. You've lost her, me boy! For every day that I work in the fireroom I'll come to her an' show her the palms of me bleedin' hands an' mention your name. An' for every day I work in the hole the hate of you will burn blacker into her heart."

"I'd rather have her hate than her pity."

"You'll have both; her hate for torturin' Harrigan; her pity for lettin' the devil in you get the best of the man. You're done for, McTee."

Each one of the short phrases was like a whip flicked across the face of McTee, but he would not wince.

"You've said enough. Now get down to the fireroom. I've had Henshaw pre-pare the chief engineer for your coming."

Harrigan turned.

"Wait! Remember when you're in hell that the old compact still holds. Your hand in mine and a promise to be my man will end the war."

Only the low laughter of the Irishman answered as he made his way down to the deck.

CHAPTER 18

"THERE'S TIMES for truth an' there's times for lying," murmured Harrigan, as he stowed away the bucket and brush and started down for the fireroom, "an' this was one of the times for lyin'. He's sick for the love of her, an' he's hatin' the thought of Harrigan."

So he was humming a rollicking tune when he reached the fireroom. It was stifling hot, to be sure, but it was twice as large as that of the Mary Rogers. The firemen were all glistening with sweat. One of them, larger than the rest and with a bristling, shoebrush mustache like a sign of authority, said to the new-comer: "You're Harrigan?"

He nodded.

"The chief wants to see you, boss, before you start swingin' the shovel."

"Where's the chief's cabin?"

"Take him up, Alex," directed the big fireman, and Harrigan followed one of the men up the narrow ladder and then aft. He was grateful for this light respite from the heat of the hole, but his joy faded when the man opened a door and he stood at last before the chief, Douglas Campbell, who looked up at the burly Irishman in a long silence.

The scion of the ancient and glorious clan of the Campbells had fallen far in-deed. His face was a brilliant red, and the nose, comically swollen at the end, was crossed with many blue veins. Like Milton's *Satan* , however, he retained some traces of his original brightness. Harrigan knew at once that the chief engineer was fully worthy of joining those rulers of the south seas and harriers of weaker men, McTee and White Henshaw.

"Stand straight and look me in the eye," said Campbell, and in his voice was a slight "bur-r-r" of the Scotch accent.

Harrigan jerked back his shoulders and stood like a soldier at attention.

"A drinkin' man," he was saying to himself, "may be hard an' fallen low, but he's sure to have a heart."

"So you're the mutineer, my fine buck?"

Harrigan hesitated, and this seemed to infuriate Campbell, who banged a brawny fist on a table and thundered: "Answer me, or I'll skin your worthless carcass!"

The cold, blue eyes of Harrigan did not falter. They studied the face of the Campbell as a fighter gauges his opponent.

"If I say 'yes,'" he responded at length, "it's as good as puttin' myself in chains; if I say 'no,' you'll be thinkin' I'm givin' in, you an' McTee, damn his eyes!"

Campbell grew still redder.

"You damn him, do you? McTee is Scotch; he's a gentleman too good to be named by swine!"

The irrepressible Harrigan replied: "He's enough to make swine speak!"

Amazement and then a gleam of laughter shone in the eyes of the chief engineer. He was seized, apparently, by a fit of violent coughing and had to turn away, hiding his face with his hand. When he faced the Irishman again, his jaw was set hard, but his eyes were moist.

"Look me in the eye, laddie. Men say a good many things about me; they call me a slave driver and worse. Why? Because when I say 'move,' my men have to jump. I've asked you a question, and I'm going to get an answer. Are you a mutineer or not?"

"I will not pleasure McTee by sayin' I'm not!"

The ponderous hand rose over the table, but it was checked before it fell.

"What the devil has McTee to do with this?" he bellowed.

"He's the one that sent me here." Harrigan was thinking fast as he went on: "And you're going to keep me here for the sake of McTee."

Campbell changed from red to purple and exploded: "I'll keep no man here to please another; not White Henshaw himself. He rules on deck, and I rule below. D'you hear? Tell me you're a liar! Speak up!"

"You're a liar," said Harrigan instantly.

The engineer's mouth opened and closed twice while he stared at Harrigan.

"Get out!" he shouted, springing to his feet. "I'll have you boxed up and sweated; I'll have you pounded to a pulp! Wait! Stay here! I'll bring in some men!"

Harrigan was desperate. He knew that what he had said was equivalent to a mutiny. He threw caution to the wind. Campbell had rung a bell.

"Bring your men an' be damned!" he answered; and now his head tilted back and he set his shoulders to the wall. "I'll be after lickin' your whole crew! A man do ye call yourself? Ah-h, ye're not fit to be lickin' the boots ay a man! Slave driver? No, ye're an overseer, an' Henshaw kicks you an' you pass the kick along. But lay a hand on Harrigan, an' he'll tear the rotten head off your shoulders!"

The door flew open, and the second assistant engineer, a burly man, with two or three others, appeared at the entrance, drawn by the furious clamor of the bell.

"What—" began the second assistant, and then stopped as he caught sight of Harrigan against the wall with his hands poised, ready for the first attack.

"Who called you?" roared Campbell.

"Your bell—" began the assistant.

"You lie! Get out! I was telling a joke to my old friend Harrigan. Maybe I leaned back against the bell. Shake hands with Harrigan. I've known him for years."

Incredulous, Harrigan lowered his clenched fist and relaxed it to meet the hesitant hand of the assistant.

"Now be off," growled the chief, and the others fled.

As the door closed, Harrigan turned in stupid amazement upon the Scotchman. The latter had dropped into his chair again and now looked at Harrigan with twinkling eyes.

"You'd have fought 'em all, eh, lad?"

He burst into heavy laughter.

"Ah, the blue devil that came in your eyes! Why did I not let them have one whirl at you? Ha, ha, ha!"

"Wake me up," muttered Harrigan. "I'm dreamin'!"

"There's a thick lie in my throat," said Campbell. "I must wash it out and leave a truth there!"

He opened a small cupboard, exposing a formidable array of black and green bottles. One of the black he pulled down, as well as two small glasses, which he filled to the brim.

"To your bonny blue eyes, lad!" he said, and raised a glass. "Here's an end to the mutiny—and a drop to our old friendship!"

Harrigan, still with clouded mind, raised the glass and drank. It was a fine sherry wine.

"How old would you say that wine was?" queried the Scotchman with exaggerated carelessness.

The carelessness did not deceive Harrigan. His mind went blanker still, for he knew little about good wines.

"Well?" asked the engineer.

"H-m!" muttered Harrigan, and racked his brain to remember the ages at which a good vintage becomes a rare old wine. "About thirty-five years."

"By the Lord!" cried Campbell. "It never fails—a strong man knows his liquor like a book! You're almost right. Add three years and you have it! Thirty-eight years in sunshine and shadow!"

He leaned back and gazed dreamily up to the ceiling.

"Think of it," he went on in a reverent murmur. "Men have been born and grown strong and then started toward the shady side of life since this wine was put in the bottle. For thirty-eight years it has been gathering and saving its perfume—draw a breath of it now, lad!—and when I uncork the bottle, all the odor blows out to me at once."

"True," said Harrigan, nodding sagely. "I've thought the same thing, but never found the words for it, chief."

"Have you?" asked Campbell eagerly. "Sit down, lad; sit down! Well, well! Good wine was put on earth for a blessing, but men have misused it, Harrigan— but hear me preaching when I ought to be praying!"

"Prayin'?" repeated the diplomatic Harrigan. "No, no, man! Maybe you've drunk a good store of liquor, but it shines through you. It puts a flush on your face like a sun shinin' through a cloud. You'd hearten any man on a dark day!"

He could not resist the play on the words, and a shadow crossed the face of the engineer.

"Harrigan," he growled, "there's a double meaning in what you say, but I'll not think of it. You're no fool, lad, but do not vex me. But say your say. I suppose I'm red enough to be seen by my own light on a dark night. What does Bobbie say?

"Oh, wad some power the giftie gie us To see oursels as others see us!"

"Well, well! I forgave you for the sake of Bobbie! Do you know his rhymes, lad?"

A light shone in the eye of Harrigan. He began to sing softly in his musical, deep voice: "Ye banks and braes of bonny Doon—"

"No, no, man!" cried Campbell, raising his hand in horror at the sound of the false accent. "It should go like this!"

He pulled a guitar out of a case and commenced to strum lightly on it, while he rendered the old song in a voice roughened by ill usage but still strong and true. A knock at the door interrupted him at the climax of his song, and he glared toward the unseen and rash intruder.

"What will ye hae?" he roared, continuing the dialect which the song had freshened on his tongue.

"The shift in the fireroom is short-handed," said the voice. "That fellow Harrigan has not shown up. Shall we search for him?"

"Search for the de'il!" thundered Campbell. "Harrigan is doing a fine piece of work for me; shall I let him go to the fireroom to swing a shovel?"

"The captain's orders, sir," persisted the voice rashly.

Campbell leaped for the door and jerked it open a few inches.

"Be off!" he cried; "or I'll set you passin' coal yourself, my fine lad! What? Will ye be asking questions? Is there no discipline? Mutiny, mutiny—that's what this is!"

"Aye, aye, sir!" murmured a rapidly retreating voice.

Campbell closed and locked the door and turned back to Harrigan with a grin.

"The world's a wide place," he said, "but there's few enough in it who know our Bobbie, God bless him! When I've found one, shall I let him go down to the fireroom? Ha! Now tell me what's wrong between you and McTee."

"I will not talk," said Harrigan with another bold stroke of diplomacy, "till I hear the rest of that song. The true Scotch comes hard on my tongue, but I'll learn it."

"You will, laddie, for your heart's right. Man, man, I'm nothing now, but you should have heard me sing in the old days—"

"When we were in Glasgow," grinned Harrigan.

"In Glasgow," repeated Campbell, and then lifted his head and finished the song. "Now for the story, laddie."

Harrigan started, as though recalled from a dream built up by the music. Then he told briefly the tale of the tyranny aboard the *Mary Rogers*, now apparently to be repeated.

"So I thought," he concluded, "that it was to be the old story over again—look at my hands!"

He held them out. The palms were still red and deeply scarred. Campbell said nothing, but his jaw set savagely.

"I thought it was to be this all over again," went on Harrigan, "till I met you, chief. But with you for a friend I'll weather the storm. McTee's a hard man, but when Scot meets Scot—I'll bet on the Campbells."

"Would you bet on me against Black McTee?" queried the engineer, deeply moved. "Well, lad, McTee's a dour man, but dour or not he shall not run the engine room of the *Heron* ."

And he banged on the table for emphasis.

"Scrub down the bridge every morning, as they tell you, but when they send you below to pass the coal, come and report to me first. I'll have work for you to do—chiefly practicing the right accent for Bobbie's songs. Is not that a man's work?"

CHAPTER 19

TO MAKE good this promise, Campbell straightway sang for Harrigan's delectation two or three more of his favorite selections. It was evening, and the shift in the fireroom was ended before Harrigan left the engineer's room. On his way to the deck he passed the tired firemen from the hole of the ship. They stared at the Irishman with wide eyes, for it was known that he had been hi the chief engineer's room for several hours; they looked upon nun as one who has been in hell and has escaped from thence to the upper air.

He was, in fact, a marked man when he reached the forecastle. Rumor travels through a ship's crew and it was already known that Black McTee hated the Irishman and that White Henshaw had commenced to persecute him in a new and terrible manner.

This would have been sufficient tragedy to burden the shoulders of any one man, however strong, and when to this was added the fact that he had been kept by the grim chief engineer for several hours in the chief's own room, and finally considering that this man had passed through a shipwreck, one of three lone survivors, it is easy to understand why the sailors gave him ample elbow room.

It was evidently expected that he would break out into a torrent of abuse, and when he, perceiving this, remained silent, their awe increased. All through supper he was aware of their wondering glances; above all he felt the gray, steady eyes of Jerry Hovey, the bos'n, yet he ate without speaking, replying to their tentative questions with grunts. Before the meal was finished and the pipes and cigarettes lighted, he was a made man. Persevering in his role, as soon as he had eaten he went out on deck and sat down in the corner between the rail and the forecastle upon a coil of rope.

As deep as the blue sea in the evening light was the peace which lay on the soul of Harrigan, for the day had brought two great victories, one over McTee and the other over the chief engineer. It was not a stolid content, for he knew the danger of the implacable hate of McTee, but with the aid of Campbell he felt that he would have a fighting chance at least to survive, and that was all he asked.

So he sat on the coil of rope leaning against the rail, and looked ahead. It was almost completely dark when a hand fell on his shoulder and he looked up into the steady, gray-blue eyes of the bos'n.

"I promised to talk to you tonight," said that worthy, and sat down uninvited on a neighboring coil of rope.

He waited for a response. As a rule, sailors are glad to curry favor with the bos'n. Harrigan, however, sat without speaking, staring through the gloom.

"Well?" said Hovey at length. "You're a silent man, Harrigan."

There was no response.

"All right; I like a silent man. In a way of speakin', I need 'em like you! If you say little to me, you're likely to say little to others.

"I don't talk much myself," went on Hovey, "until I know my man. I ain't seen much of you, but I guess I figure you straight."

He grew suddenly cautious, cunning, and the steady, gray-blue eyes reminded Harrigan of a cat when she crouches for hours watching the rathole.

"You ain't got much reason for standing in with White Henshaw?" he purred.

"H'm," grunted the Irishman, and waited.

"Sure, you ain't," went on Hovey soothingly, "because McTee has raised hell between you. They say McTee tried his damnedest to break you?"

The last question was put in a different manner; it came suddenly like a surprise blow in the dark.

"Well?" queried Harrigan. "What of it?"

"He tried all the way from Honolulu?"

"He did."

"Did he try his fists?"

"He did."

Jerry Hovey cursed with excitement.

"And?"

"I carried him to his cabin afterward," said Harrigan truthfully.

"Would you take on McTee again? Black McTee?"

"If I had to. Why?"

"Oh, nothin'. But McTee has started White Henshaw on your trail. Maybe you know what Henshaw is? The whole South Seas know him!"

"Well?"

"You'll have a sweet hell of a time before this boat touches port, Harrigan."

"I'll weather it."

"Yes, this trip, but what about the next? If Henshaw is breakin' a man, he keeps him on the ship till the man gives in or dies. I know! Henshaw'll get so much against you that he could soak you for ten years in the courts by the time we touch port. Then he'll offer to let you off from the courts if you'll ship with him again, and then the old game will start all over again. You may last one trip—other men have—one or two—but no one has ever lasted out three or four shippings under White Henshaw. It can't be done!"

He paused to let this vital point sink home. Only the same dull silence came in reply, and this continued taciturnity seemed to irritate Hovey. When he spoke again, his voice was cold and sharp.

"He's got you trapped, Harrigan. You're a strong man, but you'll never get his rope off your neck. He'll either hang you with it or else tie you hand and foot an' make you his slave. I *know!*"

There was a bitter emphasis on the last word that left no doubt as to his meaning, and Harrigan understood now the light of that steady, gray-blue eye which made the habitual smile of good nature meaningless.

"Ten years ago I shipped with White Henshaw. Ten years ago I didn't have a crooked thought or a mean one in my brain. Today there's hell inside me, understand? Hell!" He paused, breathing hard.

"There's others on this ship that have been through the same grind, some of them longer than me. There's others that ain't here, but that ain't forgotten, because me an' some of the rest, we seen them dyin' on their feet. Maybe they ain't dropped into the sea, but they're just the same, or worse. You'll find 'em loafin' along the beaches. They take water from the natives, they do."

He went on in a hoarse whisper: "On this ship I've seen 'em busted. An' Henshaw has done the bustin'. This is a coffin ship, Harrigan, an' Henshaw he's the undertaker. He don't bring 'em to Davy Jones's locker—he does worse—he brings 'em to hell on earth, a hell so bad that when they go below, they don't notice no difference. Harrigan, me an' a few of the rest, we know what's been done, an' some of us have thought wouldn't it be a sort of joke, maybe, if sometime what Henshaw has done to others was done to himself, what?"

The sweat was standing out on Harrigan's face wet and cold. It seemed to him that through the darkness he could make out whole troops of those broken men littering the decks. He peered through the dark at the bos'n, and made out the hint of the gray-blue eyes watching him again as the cat watches the mousehole, and the heart of Harrigan ached.

"Hovey, are you bound for the loincloth an' the beaches, like the rest?"

"No, because I've sold my soul to White Henshaw; but you're bound there, Harrigan, because you can never sell your soul. I looked in your eyes and seen it written there like it was in a book."

He gripped the Irishman by the shoulder.

"There's some say this is the last voyage of White Henshaw, but me an' some of the rest, we know different. He can't leave the sea, which means that he won't take us out of hell. Now, talk straight. You stood up to McTee; would you stand up to Henshaw?"

Harrigan muttered after a moment of thought: "I suppose this is mutiny, bos'n?"

"Aye, but I'm safe in talkin' it. White Henshaw trusts me, he does, because I've sold my soul to him. If you was to go an' tell nun what I've said, he'd laugh at you an' say you was tryin' to incite discontent. What's it goin' to be, Harrigan? Will you join me an' the rest who can set you free an' make a man of you, or will you stay by McTee and White Henshaw and that devil Campbell?"

"How could you set me free?"

"One move—altogether—in the night—we'd have the ship for our own, an' we could beach her and take to the shore at any place we pleased."

Harrigan repeated: "One move—altogether—in the night! I don't like it, bos'n. I'll stand up to my man foot to foot an' hand to hand, but for strikin' at him in the dark—I can't do it."

He caught the sound of Hovey's gritting teeth.

"Think it over," persisted the bos'n. "We need you, Harrigan, but if you don't join, we'll help McTee and Henshaw and Campbell to make life hell for you."

"I've thought it over. I don't like the game. This mutiny at night—it's like hittin' a man who's down."

"That's final?"

"It is."

"Then God help you, Harrigan, for you ain't the man I took you for."

CHAPTER 20

HE ROSE and left Harrigan to the dark, which now lay so thick over the sea that he could only dimly make out the black, wallowing length of the ship. After a time, he went into the dingy forecastle and stretched out on his bunk. Some of the sailors were already in bed, propping their heads up with brawny, tattooed arms while they smoked their pipes. For a time Harrigan pondered the mutiny, glancing at the stolid faces of the smokers and trying to picture them in action when they would steal through the night barefooted across the deck—some of them with bludgeons, others with knives, and all with a thirst for murder.

Sleep began to overcome him, and he fought vainly against it. In a choppy sea the bows of a ship make the worst possible bed, for they toss up and down with sickening rapidity and jar quickly from side to side; but when a vessel is plowing through a long-running ground swell, the bows of the ship move with a sway more soothing than the swing of a hammock in a wind. Under these circumstances Harrigan was lulled to sleep.

He woke at length with a consciousness, not of a light shining in his face, but of one that had just been flashed across his eyes. Then a guarded voice said: "He's dead to the world; he won't hear nothin'."

Peering cautiously up from under the shelter of his eyelashes, he made out a bulky figure leaning above him.

"Sure he's dead to the world," said a more distant voice. "After the day he must have put in with Campbell, he won't wake up till he's dragged out. I know!"

"Lift his foot and let it drop," advised another. "If you can do that to a man without waking him, you know he's not going to be waked up by any talkin'."

Harrigan's foot was immediately raised and dropped. He merely sighed as if in sleep, and continued to breathe heavily, regularly. After a moment he was conscious that the form above him had disappeared. Then very slowly he turned his head and raised his eyelids merely enough to peer through the lashes. The sailors sat cross-legged in a loose circle on the floor of the forecastle. At the four corners of the group sat four significant figures. They were like the posts of the prize ring supporting the rope; that is to say, the less important sailors who sat between them. Each of the four was a man of mark.

Facing Harrigan were Jacob Flint and Sam Hall. The former was a little man, who might have lived unnoticed forever had it not been for a terrible scar which deformed his face. It was a cut received in a knife fight at a Chinese port. The white, gleaming line ran from the top of his temple, across the side of his right eye, and down to the cheekbone. The eye was blind as a result of the wound, but in healing the cut had drawn the skin so that the lids of the eye were pulled awry in a perpetual, villainous squint. It was said that before this wound Flint had been merely an ordinary sailor, but that afterward he was inspired to live up to the terror of his deformed face.

Sam Hall, the "corner post," at Flint's right, was a type of blond stupidity, huge of body, with a bull throat and a round, featureless face. You looked in vain to find anything significant in this fellow beyond his physical strength, until your glance lingered on his eyes. They were pale blue, expressionless, but they hinted at possibilities of berserker rage.

The other two, whose backs were toward Harrigan, were Garry Cochrane and Jim Kyle. The latter might have stood for a portrait of a pirate of the eighteenth century, with a drooping, red mustache and bristling beard. The reputation of this monster, however, was far less terrible than that of any of the other three, certainly far less than Garry Cochrane. This was a lean fellow with bright black eyes, glittering like a suspicious wolf's.

Between these corner posts sat the less distinguished sailors. They might have been notable cutthroats in any other assemblage of hard-living men, but here they granted precedence willingly to the four more notable heroes.

Around the circle walked Jerry Hovey like a shepherd about his flock. It was apparent that they all held him in high favor. His chief claim to distinction, or perhaps his only one, was that he had served as bos'n for ten years under White Henshaw; but this record was enough to win the respect of even Garry Cochrane.

It was Jim Kyle who had peered into the face of Harrigan, for now he was pushing to one side the lantern he had used and settling back into his place in the circle. He gestured over his shoulder with his thumb.

"How'd you happen to miss out with the Irishman, Jerry?"

"Talk low or you may wake him," warned Hovey. "I lost him because the fool ain't sailed long enough to know White Henshaw. He has an idea that mutiny at night is like hittin' a man when he's down—as if there was any other way of hittin' Henshaw an' gettin' away with it!"

The chuckle of the sailors was like the rumble of the machinery below, blended and lost with that sound.

"So he's out—an' you know what that means," went on Hovey.

A light came into the pale eyes of Sam Hall, and his thick lips pulled back in a grin.

"Aye," he growled, "we do! He's a strong man, but"—and here he raised his vast arms and stretched them—"I'll tend to Harrigan!"

The voice of the bos'n was sharp: "None o' that! Wait till I give orders, Sam, before you raise a hand. We're too far from the coast. Let old Henshaw bring us close inshore, an' then we'll turn loose."

"What I don't see," said one of the sailors, "is how we make out for hard cash after we hit the coast. We beach the Heron—all right; but then we're turned loose in the woods without a cent."

"You're a fool," said Garry Cochrane. "We loot the ship before we abandon her. There'll be money somewhere."

"Aye," said Hovey, "there's money. That's what I got you together for tonight. There's money, and more of it than you ever dreamed of."

He waited for his words to take effect in the brains of the men, running his glance around the circle, and a light flashed in response to each eye as it met his.

He continued: "White Henshaw cashed in every cent of his property before he sailed in the *Heron* . I know, because he used me for some of his errands. And I know that he had a big safe put into his cabin. For ten years everything that White Henshaw has looked at turned into gold. I know! All that gold he's got in that safe—you can lay to that."

He turned to the sailor who had first raised the question: "Money? You'll have your share of the loot—if you can carry it!"

They drew in their breath as if they were drinking.

Hovey continued: "Now, lads, I know you're gettin' excited and impatient. That's why I've got you together. You've got to wait. And until I give the word, you've got to keep your eyes on the deck an' run every time one of the mates of White Henshaw—damn his heart!—gives the word. Why? Because one wrong word—one queer look—will tip off the skipper that something's wrong, and once he gets suspicious, you can lay to it that he'll find out what we're plannin'. I *know!*"

There was a grim significance in that repeated phrase, "I *know* ," for it hinted at a knowledge more complete and evil than falls to the share of the ordinary mortal.

"Lads, keep your eyes on the deck and play the game until I give the word! If the wind of this comes to the captain, it's overboard for Jerry Hovey. I'd rather give myself to the sharks than to White Henshaw. That's all.

"Now, lads, it's come to the point where we've got to know what we'll do. There's two ways. One is to crowd all them what ain't in the mutiny into one cabin an' keep 'em there till we beach the boat."

"So that they can get out and tell the land sharks what we've done?" suggested Garry Cochrane in disgust.

"Garry," said Hovey with deep feeling, "you're a lad after my heart. And you're right. If one of them lives, he'll be enough to put a halter around the necks of each of us. We couldn't get away. If we're once described, there ain't no way we could dodge the law."

He grinned sardonically as he looked about the circle: "There's something about us, lads, that makes us different from other men."

The sailors glanced appreciatively at the scarred countenances of their fellows and laughed hoarsely.

"So the second way is the only way," went on Hovey, seeing that he had scored his point. "The rest of the crew that ain't with us has got to go under. Are you with me?"

"Aye," croaked the chorus, and every man looked down at the floor. Each one had picked out the man he hated the most, and was preparing the manner of the killing.

"Good," said Hovey; "and now that we've agreed on that, we've got to choose—"

He stopped, going rigid and blank of face. He had seen the open, chilling blue eye of Harrigan, who, drawn on into forgetfulness, had lain for some time on his bunk watching the scene without caution.

CHAPTER 21

"HE'S HEARD!" stammered Hovey, pointing. "Guard the door! Get him!"

"Bash in his head an' overboard with the lubber!" growled Sam Hall.

Not one of the others spoke; their actions were the more significant. Some leaped to the door and barred the exit.

Others started for Harrigan. The latter leaped off his bunk and, sweeping up a short-legged, heavy stool, sprang back against the wall. This he held poised, ready to drive it at the first man who approached. Their semicircle grew compact before him, but still they hesitated, for the man who made the first move would die.

"You fools!" said Harrigan, brandishing his stool. "Keep off!"

He was thinking desperately, quickly.

"Harrigan," said Hovey, edging his way to the front of the sailors, "you heard!"

"I did!"

They growled, infuriated. His death was certain now, but they kept back for another moment, astonished that this man would sign his own sentence of doom. From marlinspikes to pocketknives, every man held some sort of a weapon. Garry Cochrane, flattening himself against the wall at one side, edged inch by inch toward Harrigan.

"I heard it all," said the Irishman, "and until the last word I thought you were a lot of bluffin' cowards."

"You had your chance, Harrigan," said Hovey, "an' you turned me down. Now you get what's due you."

The sailors crouched a little as if at a command to leap forward in the attack. Cochrane was perilously near.

"If I get my due," said Harrigan coolly, "you'll go down on your knees. Stand back, Cochrane, or I'll brain ye! You'll go down on your knees an' thank God that I'm with ye!"

"Stand fast, Garry!" ordered Hovey. "What do you mean, Harrigan?"

The Irishman laughed. Every son of Erin is an actor, and now Harrigan's laughter rang true.

"What should I mean except what I said?" he answered.

"He's tryin' to save his head," broke in Kyle, "but with the fear of death lookin' him in the eye, any man would join us. Finish him, lads."

"You fool!" said Harrigan authoritatively. "Don't talk so loud, or you'll have White Henshaw down on our heads. Maybe he's heard that bull voice of yours already!"

It was a master stroke. The mention of the terrible skipper and the skillful insinuation that he was one of them, made them straighten and stare at him.

"Go guard the door," said Hovey to one of his sailors, "an' see that none of the mates is near. Now, Harrigan, what d'you mean? You'd hear no word of mutiny when I talked to you. Speak for your life now, because we're hard to convince."

"We can't be convinced," said Garry Cochrane, "but maybe it'll be fun to hear him talk before we dump him overboard."

Instead of answering the speaker, Harrigan looked upon Hovey with a cold eye of scorn.

He said: "I changed my mind. I'm *not* one of you. I thought the bos'n was a real captain for the gang, but I'll not follow a dog that lets every one of his pack yelp."

"I'm a dog, am I?" snarled Hovey furiously. "I'll teach you what I am, Harrigan. An' you, Cochrane, keep your face shut. I'll learn you who's boss of this little crew!"

"If you're half the man you seem," went on Harrigan, "this game looks good to me."

"You lie," said the bos'n. "You turned me down cold when I talked to you."

"You fool, that was because you said no word outright of wipin' out the officers an' takin' control of the ship. You sneaked up to me in the dark; you felt me out before you said a word; you were like a cat watchin' a rathole. Am I a rat? Am I a sneak? Do I have to be whispered to? No, I'm Harrigan, an' anyone who wants to talk to me has got to speak out like a man!"

The very impudence of his speech held them in check for another precious moment. He whirled the heavy stool.

"If you wanted me, why didn't you come an' say: 'Harrigan, I know you. You hate Henshaw an' McTee an' the rest. We're goin' to wipe 'em out an' beach the ship. Are you with us?' Why, then I'd of shook hands with you, and that would end it. But when you come whisperin' and insinuatin', sayin' nothin' straight from the shoulder, how'd I know you weren't sent by Henshaw to feel me out, eh? How do any of you know the bos'n ain't feelin' you out for the skipper he's sailed with ten years?"

The circle shifted, loosened; half the men were facing Hovey with suspicious eyes. They had not thought of this greater danger, and the bos'n was desperate in the crisis.

"Boys," he pleaded, "are you goin' to let one stranger ball up our game? Are you goin' to start doubtin' me on his say-so?"

The men glanced from him to Harrigan. Plainly they were deep in doubt, and the Irishman made his second masterful move. He stepped forward, dropping his stool with a crash to the floor, and clapped a hand upon Hovey's shoulder.

"I spoke too quick," he said frankly, "but you got me mad, bos'n. I know you're straight, an' I'm with you, for one. A man Harrigan will toiler ought to be good enough for the rest, eh?"

Jerry Hovey wiped his gleaming forehead. The kingdom of his ambition was rebuilt by this speech.

"Sit down, boys," he ordered. "The last man in the forecastle is with us now. We're solid. Sit down and we'll plan our game."

The plan, as it developed after the circle re-formed, was a simple one. They were to wait until the ship was within two or three days' voyage from the coast of Central America—their destination—and then they would act. They had secured to their side the firemen and the first assistant engineer. That meant that they could run the ship safely with the bos'n, who understood navigation, at the wheel. They would select a night, and then, on the command of Hovey, the men would take the arms which they had prepared.

One of the Japanese cabin boys, Kamasura, was a member of the plot. He would furnish butcherknives and cleavers from the kitchen. Besides this, there were various implements which could be used as bludgeons; and finally there were the pocketknives with which every sailor is always equipped, generally stout, long-bladed instruments. The advantage of firearms was with the officers of the ship, but apparently there were no rifles and probably very few revolvers aboard. Against powder and lead they would have the advantage of a surprise attack.

First, Sam Hall and Kyle were to go down to the hole of the ship and lead the firemen in their attack upon the oilers and wipers, most of whom had not been approachable with the plan of mutiny because they were newly signed on the ship. In this part of the campaign the most important feature would be the capturing of Campbell, who would be reserved for a finely drawn-out, tortured death. The firemen had insisted upon this.

In the meantime Hovey with Flint and the rest would attack the cabins of Henshaw, McTee, and the mates. Here they depended chiefly upon the effect of the surprise. If it were possible, Henshaw also was to be taken alive and reserved for a long death like Campbell. This done, they would lead the ship to an uninhabited part of the shore, beach her, and scatter over the mainland, each with his share of the booty.

Harrigan forced himself to take an active part in the discussion of the plans. Several features were his own suggestion, among others the idea of presenting a petition for better food to Henshaw, and beating him down while he was reading it; but all the time that the Irishman spoke, he was thinking of Kate.

When the crew turned into their bunks at last, he went over a thousand schemes in his head. In the first place he might go to Henshaw at once and warn him of the coming danger, but he remembered what the bos'n had said—in such a case he would not be believed, and both the crew and the commander would be against him.

Finally it seemed to him that the best thing was to wait until the critical moment had arrived. He could warn the captain just in time—or if absolutely necessary he could warn McTee, who would certainly believe him. In the mean-time there were possibilities that the mutiny would come to nothing through internal dissension among the crew. In any case he must play a detestable part, acting as a spy upon the crew and pretending enthusiasm for the mutiny.

With that shame like a taste of soot in his throat, he climbed to the bridge the next morning with his bucket of suds and his brush, and there as usual he found McTee, cool and clean in the white outfit of Henshaw. At sight of the Scotchman he remembered at once that he must pretend the double exhaustion which comes of pain and hard labor. Therefore he thrust out his lower jaw and favored McTee with a glare of hate. He was repaid by the glow of content which showed in the captain's face.

"And the hole of the *Heron* ," he said, speaking softly lest his voice should carry to the man in the wheelhouse, "is it cooler than the fireroom of the *Mary Rogers?* "

Harrigan glanced up, glowering.

"Damn you, McTee!"

"The palms of your hands, lad, are they raw? Is the lye of the suds cool to them?"

Another black glance came in reply and McTee leaned back against the rail, tapping one contented toe against the floor.

"It was a fine tale you told me yesterday, Harrigan," he said at length, "but afterward I saw Kate, and she was never kinder. I spoke of you, and we laughed together about it. She said you were like a horse that's too proud—you need the whip!"

Harrigan was in doubt, but he concealed his trouble with a mighty effort and smiled.

"That's a weak lie, Angus. When I was a boy of ten, I would of hung me head for shame if I could not have made a better lie. Shall I tell you what really happened when you met Kate? You came up smilin' an' grinnin' like a baboon, an' she passed you by with a look that went through you as if you were just a cloud on the edge of the sky. Am I right, McTee?"

"You've seen her, and she's told you this," exclaimed the captain.

Harrigan chuckled his triumph and went on with the scrubbing of the bridge.

"No, Angus, me dear, I've not seen her, but when two souls are as close as hers and mine—well, cap'n, I leave it to you!"

McTee ground his teeth with rage and turned his back on the worker for a moment until he could master the contorted muscles of his face.

"Tut, McTee," went on the Irishman, "you've but felt the tickle of the spur; when I drive it in, you'll yell like a whipped kid. Always you play into me hands, McTee. Now when you see Kate, you'll feel me grin in the background mockin' ye, eh?"

The banter gave the captain a shrewd inspiration. He leaned, and catching one of Harrigan's hands with a quick movement, turned it palm up. It was as he suspected; the palm, though red from the effect of the strong suds and still scarcely healed after the torment of the *Mary Rogers*, was nevertheless manifestly unharmed by the labor which it was supposed Harrigan had performed the day before. The hand was wrenched away and a balled fist held under McTee's nose.

"If you're curious, Angus, look at me knuckles, not me palm. It's the knuckles you'll feel the most, cap'n."

CHAPTER 22

BUT MCTEE, deep in thought, was walking from the bridge. He went straight to the hole of the ship and questioned some of the firemen, and they told him that Harrigan had done no work passing coal the day before; Campbell, it appeared, had taken him for some special job. With this tidings the Scotchman hastened back to Henshaw.

"The game's slipping through our hands, captain," he said.

"Harrigan?" queried Henshaw.

"Aye. He didn't pass a shovelful of coal in the hole yesterday."

"Tut, tut," answered the other with a wave of the hand. "I sent orders to Campbell, and told him what sort of a man he could expect to find in Harrigan."

"I've just talked to the firemen. They say that Harrigan didn't handle a single pound of coal. That ought to be final."

Henshaw went black.

"It may be so. I've given more rope to old Campbell than to any man that ever sailed the seas with White Henshaw, and it may be he's using the rope now to hang himself. We'll find out, McTee; we'll find out! Where's Harrigan now?"

"Gone below a while ago after he finished scrubbing down the bridge."

"We'll speak with Douglas. Come along, McTee. There's nothing like discipline on the high seas."

He went below, murmuring to himself, with McTee close behind him. Strange sounds were coming from the room of the chief engineer, sounds which seemed much like the strumming of a guitar.

"He's playing his songs," grinned Henshaw, and he chuckled noiselessly. "Listen! We'll give him something to sing about—and it'll be in another key. Ha-ha!"

He tasted the results of his disciplining already, but just as he placed his hand on the knob of the door, another sound checked him and made him turn with a puzzled frown toward McTee. It was a ringing baritone voice which rose in an Irish love song.

"What the devil—" began Henshaw.

"You're right," nodded McTee. "It's the devil—Harrigan. Open the door!"

The captain flung it open, and they discovered the two worthies seated at ease with a black bottle and two glasses at hand. Campbell, in the manner of a musical critic of some skill, leaned back in a chair with his brawny arms folded behind his head and his eyes half closed. Harrigan, tilted back hi a chair, rested his feet on the edge of a small table and swept the guitar which lay on his lap. In the midst of a high note he saw the ominous pair standing in the door, and the music died abruptly on his lips.

He rose to his feet and nudged Campbell at the same time. The latter opened his eyes and, glimpsing the unwelcome visitors, sprang up, gasping, stammering.

"What? Come in! Don't be standing there, Cap'n Henshaw. Come in and sit down!"

In spite of his bluster his red face was growing blotched with patches of gray. Harrigan, less moved than any of the others, calmly replaced the guitar in its green cloth case.

"I sent this fellow down to be put at hard work," said Henshaw, and waited.

It was obvious to Harrigan that the chief engineer was in mortal fear. He himself felt strangely ill at ease as he looked at White Henshaw with his skin yellow as Egyptian papyrus from a tomb.

"Just a minute, captain," began the engineer. "You sent Harrigan down to the hole because he's considered a hard man to handle, eh?"

Henshaw waited for a fuller explanation; he seemed to be enjoying the distress of Campbell.

"Just so," went on the Scotchman, "but there are two ways of handling a difficult sailor. One is by using the club and the other by using kindness. The club has been tried and hasn't worked very well with Harrigan. I decided to take a hand with kindness. The results have been excellent. I was just about—"

His voice died away, for McTee was chuckling in a deep bass rumble, and Henshaw was smiling in a way that boded no good.

The captain broke in coldly: "I've heard enough of your explanation, Campbell. Send Harrigan down to the hole at once. We'll work him a double shift today, for a starter."

Campbell was trembling like a self-conscious girl, for he was drawn between shame and dread of the captain.

"Look!" he cried, and taking the hand of Harrigan, he turned it palm up. "This chap has been brutally treated. He's been at work that fairly tore the skin from the palms of his hands. One hour's work with a shovel, captain, would make Harrigan useless at any sort of a job for a month."

"Which goes to show," said McTee, "that you don't know Harrigan."

"I've heard what you have to say," said Henshaw. "I sent him down to work hi the hole; I come down and find him singing in your room. I expect you to have him passing coal inside of fifteen minutes, Campbell."

Harrigan started for the door, feeling that the game had been played out, and glad of even this small respite of a day or more from the labor of the shovel. Before he left the room, however, the voice of Campbell halted him.

"Wait! Stay here! You'll do what I tell you, Harrigan. I'm the boss below-decks."

It was a declaration of war, and what it cost Campbell no one could ever tell. He stood swaying slightly from side to side, while he glared at Henshaw.

"You're drunk," remarked the captain coldly. "I'll give you half an hour, Campbell, to come to your senses—but after that—"

"Damn you and your time! I want no tune! I say the lad has been put through hell and shan't go back to it, do you hear me?"

Henshaw was controlling himself carefully, or else he wished to draw out the engineer.

He said: "You know the record of Harrigan?"

"What record? The one McTee told you? Would you believe what Black McTee says of a man he tried to break and couldn't?"

"My friend McTee is out of the matter. All that you have to do with is my order. You've heard that order, Campbell!"

"I'll see you in hell before I send him to the hole."

Henshaw waited another moment, quietly enjoying the wild excitement of the engineer like the Spanish gentleman who sits in safety in the gallery and watches the baiting of the bull in the arena below.

"I shall send that order to you in writing. If you refuse to obey then, I shall act!"

He turned on his heel; McTee stayed a moment to smile upon Harrigan, and then followed. As the door closed, Harrigan turned to Campbell and found him sitting, shuddering, with his face buried in his hands. He touched the Scotch-man on the shoulder.

"You've done your part, chief. I won't let you do any more. I'm starting now for the hole."

"What?" bellowed Campbell. "Am I no longer the boss of my engine room? You'll sit here till I tell you to move! Damn Henshaw and his written orders!"

"If you refuse to obey a written order, he can take your license away from you in any marine court."

"Let it go."

"Ah-h, chief, ye're afther bein' a thrue man an' a bould one, but I'd rather stay the rest av me life in the hole than let ye ruin yourself for me. Whisht, man, I'm goin'! Think no more av it!"

Campbell's eyes grew moist with the temptation, but then the fighting blood of his clan ran hot through his veins.

"Sit down," he commanded. "Sit down and wait till the order comes. It's a fine thing to be chief engineer, but it's a better thing to be a man. What does Bobbie say?"

And he quoted in a ringing voice: "A man's a man for a' that!" Afterward they sat in silence that grew more tense as the minutes passed, but it seemed that Henshaw, with demoniac cunning, had decided to prolong the agony by delaying his written order and the consequent decision of the engineer. And Harrigan, watching the suffused face of Campbell, knew that the time had come when his will would not suffice to make him follow the dictates of his conscience.

All of which Henshaw knew perfectly well as he sat in his cabin filling the glass of McTee with choice Scotch.

They sat for an hour or more, chatting, and McTee drew a picture of the pair waiting below in silent dread—a picture so vivid that Henshaw laughed hi his breathless way. In time, however, he decided that they had delayed long enough, and took up pen and paper to write the order which was to convince the dauntless Campbell that even he was a slave. As he did so, Sloan, the wireless operator, appeared at the door, saying: "The report has come, sir."

CHAPTER 23

HE HELD a little folded paper in his hand. At sight of it Henshaw turned in his chair and faced Sloan with a wistful glance.

"Good?"

"Not very, sir."

Henshaw rose slowly and frowned like the king on the messenger who bears tidings of the lost battie.

"Then very bad?"

"I'm afraid so."

"Very well. Let me have the message. You may go."

He took the slip of paper cautiously, as if it were dangerous in itself, and then called back the operator as the latter reached the door.

"Come back a minute. Sloan, you're a good boy—a very good boy. Faithful, intelligent; you know your business. H-m! Here—here's a five spot"—he slipped the money into Sloan's hand—"and you shall have more when we touch port. Now this message, my lad—you couldn't have made any mistake in receiving it? You couldn't have twisted any of the words a little?"

"No mistake, I'm sure, sir. It was repeated twice."

"That makes it certain, then—certain," muttered Henshaw. "That is all, Sloan."

As the latter left the cabin, the old captain went back to his chair and sat with the paper resting upon his knee, as if a little delay might change its import.

"I am growing old, McTee," he said at last, apologetically, "and age affects the eyes first of all. Suppose you take this message, eh? And read it through to me—slowly—I hate fast reading, McTee."

The big Scotchman took the slip of paper and read with a long pause between each word:

Beatrice—failing—rapidly—hemorrhage—this—morning—very—weak.

The paper was snatched from his hand, and Henshaw repeated the words over and over to himself: "Weak—failing—hemorrhage—the fools! A little bleeding at the nose they call a hemorrhage!"

McTee broke in: "A good many doctors are apt to make a case seem more serious than it is. They get more credit that way for the cure, eh?"

"God bless you, lad! Aye, they're a lot of damnable curs! Burning at sea— death by fire at sea! He was right! The old devil was right! Look, McTee! I'm safe on my ship; I'm rich; but still I'm burning to death in the middle of the ocean."

He shook the Scotchman by his massive shoulder.

"Go get Sloan—bring him here!"

McTee rose.

"No! Don't let me lay eyes on him—he brought me this! Go yourself and carry him a message to send. The doctors are letting her die; they think she has no money. Send them this message:

" *Save Beatrice at all costs. Call in the greatest doctors. I will pay all bills ten times over.* "

"Quick! Why are you waiting here? You fool! Run! Minutes mean life or death to her!"

McTee hastened back to the wireless house in the after-part of the ship. To Sloan he gave the message, even exaggerating it somewhat. After it was sent, he said: "Look here, my boy, do you realize that it's dangerous to bring the captain messages like that last one you carried to him?"

"Do I know it? I should say I do! Once the old boy jumped at me like a tiger because I carried in a bad report."

"Could you make up a false message?"

"It's against the law, sir."

"It's not against the law to keep a man from going crazy."

"Crazy?"

"I mean what I say. Henshaw is balancing on the ragged edge of insanity. Mark my words! If the news comes of his granddaughter's death, he'll fall on the other side. Why can't you give him some hope in the meantime? Suppose you work up something this afternoon like this: 'Beatrice rallying rapidly. Doctor's much more hopeful.' What do you say?"

"Crazy!" repeated the wireless operator, fascinated. "If the old man loses his reason, we're all in danger."

"He's on the verge of it. I know something of this subject. I've studied it a lot. A common sign is when one fancy occupies a man's brain. Henshaw has two of them. One is what an old soothsayer told him: that he would die by fire at sea; the other is his love for this girl. Between the two, he's hi bad shape. Remember that he's an old man."

"You're right, sir; and I'll do it. It may not be legal, but we can't stop for law in a case like this."

McTee nodded and went back to Henshaw, whom he found walking the cabin with a step surprisingly elastic and quick.

"Go back and send another message," he called. "I made a mistake. I didn't send one that was strong enough. They may not understand. What I should have said was—"

"I made it twice as strong as the way you put it," said McTee; and he repeated his phrasing of the message with some exaggeration.

The lean hand of the captain wrung his.

"You're a good lad, McTee—a fine fellow. Stand by me. You'd never guess how my brain is on fire; the old devil of a soothsayer was right. But that message you sent will bring those deadheaded doctors to life. Ah, McTee, if I were only there for a minute in spirit, I could restore her to life—yes, one minute!"

"Of course you could. But in the meantime, for a change of thought, suppose you finish that order you were about to write out and send to Campbell."

"What order?"

"About Harrigan."

"Who the devil is Harrigan?"

McTee drew a deep breath and answered quietly: "The man you ordered to work in the hole. Here's the paper and your pen."

He placed them in the hands of the captain, but the latter held them idly.

"It's the frail ones who are carried off by the white plague. Am I right?"

"No, you're wrong. The frail ones sometimes have a better chance than the husky people. Look at the number of athletes who are carried away by it!"

"God bless you, McTee!"

"The strength that counts is the strength of spirit, and this girl has your own fighting spirit."

"Do you think so?"

"Yes; I saw it in her eyes."

Henshaw shook his head sadly.

"No; they're the eyes of her grandmother, and she had no fighting spirit. I think I married her more for pity than for love. Her grandmother died by that same disease, McTee."

The latter gave up the struggle and spent an hour soothing the excited old man. When he managed to escape, he went up and down the deck breathing deeply of the fresh air. For the moment Harrigan was safe, but it would not be long before he would force Henshaw to deliver the order. Into this reverie broke the voice of Jerry Hovey.

"Beg your pardon, Captain McTee."

The Scotchman turned to the bos'n with the smile still softening his stern lips.

"Well?" he asked good-naturedly.

"Let me have half a dozen words, sir."

"A thousand, bos'n. What is it?"

Now, Hovey remembered what Harrigan had said about coming straight to the point, and he appreciated the value of the advice. Particularly in speaking to a man like McTee, for he recognized in the Scotchman some of the same strong, blunt characteristics of Harrigan.

"Every man who's sailed the South Seas knows Captain McTee," he began.

"None of that, lad. If you know me, you also know that I'm called Black McTee—and for a reason."

"More than that, sir, we know that whatever men say of you, your word has always been good."

"Well?"

"I'm going to ask you to give me your word that what I have to say, if it doesn't please you, will go out one ear as fast as it goes in the other."

"You have my word."

"And maybe your hand, sir?"

McTee, stirred by curiosity, shook hands.

Hovey began: "Some of us have sailed a long time and never got much in the pocket to show for it."

"Yes, that's true of me."

"But there's none of us would turn our backs on the long green?"

McTee grinned.

"Well, sir, I have a little plan. Suppose you knew an old man—a man so old, sir, that he was sure to die in a year or so. And suppose he had one heir—a girl who was about to die—"

"Mutiny, bos'n," said McTee coldly.

But the eye of Hovey was fully as cold; he knew his man.

"Well?" he queried.

"Talk ahead. I've given you my word to keep quiet."

"Suppose this old man had a lot of money. Would it be any crime—any great crime to slip a little of that long green into our pockets?"

Two pictures were in McTee's mind—one of the safe piled full of gold, and the other of the half-crazed old skipper with his dying granddaughter. After all, it was only a matter of months before Henshaw would be dead, for certainly he would not long survive the death of Beatrice. Even a small portion of that hoard would enable him to leave the sea—to woo Kate as she must be wooed before he could win her. Golden would be the veil with which he could blind her eyes to the memory of Harrigan after he had removed the Irishman from his path.

"Very well, bos'n. I understand what you mean. I've seen the inside of that safe in the cabin. Now I come straight to the point. Why do you talk with me?"

"Because I need a man like you."

"To lead the mutiny?"

"Tell me first, are you with us?"

"Who are us?"

"You'll have to speak first."

"I'm with you."

"Now I'll tell you. The whole forecastle is hungry for the end of White Henshaw. Your share of the money is whatever you want to make it. You can have all my part; what I want is the sight of Henshaw crawlin' at our feet."

"You're a good deal of a man, Hovey. Henshaw has put you in his school, and now you're about to graduate, eh? But why do you want me? What brought you to me?"

"I thought I didn't need you a while ago; now I have to have somebody stronger than I am. I was the king of the bunch yesterday; but the last man we took into our plan proved to be stronger than I am."

"Who?"

"Harrigan."

McTee straightened slowly and his eyes brightened. Hovey went on: "Before he'd been with us ten minutes, the rest of the men in the forecastle were looking up to him. He has the reputation. He won it by facing you and Henshaw at the same time. Now the lads listen to me, but they keep their eyes on Harrigan. I know what that means. That's why I come here and offer the leadership to you."

McTee was thinking rapidly.

"A plan like this is fire, bos'n, and I have an idea I might burn my fingers unless you have enough of the crew with you. If you have Harrigan, it certainly means that you have a majority of the rest."

Hovey grinned: "Aye, you know Harrigan."

The insinuation made McTee hot, but he went on seriously: "If you could make me sure that you have Harrigan, I'd be one of you."

"What proof do you want?"

"None will do except the word out of his own mouth. Listen! Along about four bells this afternoon I'll find some way of sending Miss Malone out of her cabin. Then I'll go in there and wait. Bring Harrigan close to that door at that tune and make him talk about the mutiny. Can you do it?"

"But why the room of the girl?"

"You're stupid, Hovey. Because if you talked outside of the cabin where I sleep—that being the office of Henshaw—he'd hear you as well as I would."

"Then I'll bring him to the door of the girl's cabin. At four bells?"

"Right."

"After that we'll talk over the details, sir?"

"We will. And keep away from me, Hovey. If Henshaw sees me talking with members of his crew, he might begin to think—and any of his thinking is dangerous for the other fellow."

The bos'n touched his cap.

"Aye, aye, sir. You can begin hearin' the chink of the money, and I begin to see White Henshaw eatin' dirt. With Black McTee—excusin' the name, sir—to lead us, there ain't nothin' can stop us."

CHAPTER 24

HE WENT off toward the forecastle hitching at his trousers and whistling an old English song of the Spanish Main. As for Black McTee, he remained staring after Hovey with a rising thought of perjury. The loot of the *Heron* was a deep temptation, and his pledged word to the bos'n was a strong bond, for as Hovey had said, the honor of Black McTee, in spite of his other failings, was respected throughout the South Seas. For one purpose, however, he would have sacrificed all hopes of plunder and a thousand plighted words, and that purpose was the undoing of Harrigan in the eyes of Kate.

She had grown into a necessity to him. Though were she twice as beautiful, he would never have paid her the dangerous honor of a second glance under ordinary conditions, but their life together on the island and his rivalry with Harrigan for her sake had made her infinitely dear to him.

Seeing the opportunity to destroy all her respect for Harrigan, he schemed instantly to betray his word to Hovey. Like Harrigan earlier in the day, he had no purpose to reveal the planned mutiny at once. The Irishman waited because he did not know to whom he could confide the dangerous information; McTee delayed hi the hope of nipping insurrection in the bud at the very instant when it was about to flower. It would be far more spectacular. Moreover, he saw in this a manner of enlisting Kate on his side.

Shortly before four bells in the afternoon he went to her cabin and knocked at the door. When she opened it to him, she stood with one hand upon the knob, blocking the way and waiting silently for an explanation of his coming. That quiet coldness banished from his mind the speech which he had prepared.

He said at last: "Kate, I want you to talk with me for a few minutes."

She considered him seriously—without fear, but with such a deep distrust that he was startled. He had not dreamed that matters had progressed as far as that. At length she stepped back, and without a word beckoned him to come inside. He entered and then his eyes raised and met her glance with such a deep, still yearning that she was startled. No woman can see the revelation of a man's love without being moved to the heart.

She said: "You are in trouble, Angus?"

The hunger of his eyes came full in her face.

"Aye, trouble."

"And you have come to me—" she asked; and before she could finish her sentence, McTee broke in, pleadingly:

"For help."

He saw her lips part, her eyes brighten; he knew it was his despair which was winning her.

"Tell me!" And she made a little gesture with both hands toward him.

"I have seen it for days. I have lost all hope of you, Kate."

Her glance wandered slightly, and his hope increased.

"Because of Harrigan," he said.

She was remembering what Harrigan had said: "How to stop McTee? Make yourself old and your skin yellow, and your hair gray, and take the spring out of your step."

"Why do you keep the whip over him, Angus? He has saved your life, and you his. Why will you not treat him as one strong and generous man would treat another?"

"Because I love you, Kate."

"Angus, would you stop if you knew I loved him?"

"Is that a fair question, Kate? Even if you said you loved him, I could not stop, because I would have to do my best to save you from yourself."

She looked her query silently.

"He is not worthy of you, Kate. Because he seems generous and simple, do not be deceived. He is capable of things which even Black McTee would turn from. I know it, for I know his type. But I, Kate—your head is turned; do you hear me?"

She rose and cried: "Why have you both thought from the first that I must choose between you? Are there no other men in the whole world?"

He answered doggedly: "You will never find another who will love you as we do. To one of us you must finally belong."

"And that is why you go ahead with your schemes to torture Harrigan, certain that when he is finished I will be helpless?"

"No, I am certain of nothing. But I am absolutely sure that Harrigan stands between you and me, and I will have him done for."

"Let me think, Angus. You have pulled my old world about my ears, and now I am trying to build another kingdom where force is the only god. Can there be such a place?"

Four bells sounded. He wondered if Hovey would bring Harrigan at the time they had agreed upon. And she stood with her hands pressed against her eyes, trembling.

"In one thing at least you spoke the truth, Angus. There are only two men left for me in the world. I must choose between you and Harrigan."

"Until that time comes, I must fight for you, Kate, in the only way I know how to fight—with both my hands, trying to kill the things that stand between us—Hush!"

For he heard the rumble of two deep voices near the door.

CHAPTER 25

KATE AND McTee both stood frozen with attention, for one of the voices was Harrigan's, saying: "And why the devil have you brought me away up here, bos'n?"

"Because we have to watch sharp, Harrigan. There are some of the lads we can't trust too far, and they mustn't overhear us when we talk."

"Why, Hovey, they can hear us inside the cabin."

"She cannot. This is the girl's cabin, and I saw her go out a while ago."

"Well, then, what is it you want to know?"

"I'll tell you, man to man. When you said you were with us last night, I've been thinking you might have said it for fear of the lads."

"Hovey, you're thick in the head. Didn't you hear me talk?"

"I did, and I may be thick in the head, but I can't rest easy till you give me your hand and tell me you're playin' straight with us. You were backward at first, Harrigan."

There was an instant of pause, and then Harrigan answered: "I can't take your hand, Hovey."

McTee set his teeth. To have his plans upset when all so far had gone with perfect smoothness was maddening.

"Why not?" asked Hovey sharply.

"It's just a queer hunch I've always had. I don't like the idea of takin' any oath. I'm a man of action, Hovey. When the night comes, give me a club, and you'll see where I stand!"

There was a subdued, purring danger in his voice which made Kate tremble. Evidently it convinced Hovey.

"I guess you're right, Harrigan. I don't want to doubt you; God knows we got a need for men like you when the time comes. The other lads think there'll be nothin' to it, but I know Henshaw—I *know!*"

"It'll be a hard nut to crack. I don't make any mistake about that," said Harrigan; "but if we work cool and with a rush, we'll sweep them off their feet."

"Now you're talkin'," said Hovey. "Speed is the thing we want most. Speed, and no quarter."

"You'll need no urging for that. The boys are all set to kill. Have the officers many revolvers?"

"Not many. Salvain has one, and so has Henshaw. I don't think the rest pack any. Harrigan, I've got a weight off my mind, knowing that you're sure with us. And you'll get any share of the loot you want to name."

There was another brief pause.

"I'm easy satisfied," said Harrigan. "What I want is that the girl who has this cabin—Kate Malone—should be handled with gloves."

"Ah, there speaks the Irish!"

"I want the care of her to fall to my hands."

"Aye, you could have ten like her, as far as I'm concerned."

"Then I'm your man, Hovey. There comes one of the mates. Let's move on."

"Right-o, lad."

Their voices retreated, and after a time McTee looked down at Kate. She was dazed, as if someone had struck her in the face.

"What does it mean, Angus?"

"Wasn't it plain? Mutiny!"

She struck her hand sharply across her forehead with a little moan.

"I warned you, Kate, that he was capable of anything, but I never dreamed of a proof coming as quickly as this."

"I can't believe it; I won't believe it."

He shrugged his shoulders.

"Why should I blame him?" he said. "He sees a way to get you. I could almost sink as low as that myself—but not quite—not quite! I know something of mutinies at sea. Have you noticed the fellows who are in this crew?"

"I don't know—yes—I'm too sick to remember a single face except one scar-faced man."

"On the whole they're the roughest lot I've ever seen cooped up together. If they should be turned loose, they would make a shambles of this ship—a red shambles, Kate!"

There was not a trace of color in her face. She watched him with a horrified fascination.

"Of course," he went on easily, "I'll be the first one to go down. Harrigan would see to that. Well, it would be a worthwhile fight—while I lasted!"

"It can never take place!" she said desperately. "You are forewarned. Tell Captain Henshaw at once, and—"

He raised his hand solemnly.

"You must not do that, Kate. You must promise me not to speak a word on the subject until I have given you leave."

"I will promise you anything—but why not speak of it at once? I feel as if we were standing over a—a magazine of powder!"

"We are—only worse. But it would be madness to warn Henshaw now. He is unnerved—almost insane. His granddaughter, for whom he had made all his fortune and to whom he is going in the States—"

"Yes, Salvain told me. She is dying; it is pitiful, Angus, but—"

"He must not be told. He would start with the hand of iron, and the first act of violence which he committed would be the touch of fire which would set off this powder magazine. No, we must wait. Perhaps in a little time I may be able to win over one of the mutineers and from him learn all their plans, and then turn the tables on them. But I must first know all the men who are concerned in the uprising. When we *do* move—shall I spare Harrigan, Kate?"

He tried to ask it frankly, but a devil of malice was in his eyes.

"I don't know—I can't think! Angus, what did Dan mean?"

"I warned you of what he was capable," he said.

She caught his hands, stammering: "You are all that is left to me. You will stand between me and danger, Angus? You will protect me? But wait! I could go to Harrigan. I *know* that if I plead with him, I can win him away from the mutineers!"

"Kate, you are hysterical! Don't you see that a man who is capable of planning a wholesale murder in the night would be quite able to lie to you? No, no! Whatever you do, you must promise me not to speak a word of this to anyone, most of all, to Harrigan."

"I will promise anything—I will do anything. It all rests with you, Angus."

84

"And when we strike at the mutineers—if Harrigan falls, will you absolve me of his death, Kate?"

She was terribly moved, standing stiff and straight and helpless like a child about to be punished.

"Angus, for the sake of pity, do not ask me."

"I must know."

"Angus," came her broken voice, "I *cannot* give up my faith in him."

His face grew as dark as night, but he laid a gentle hand on her shoulder and said: "Your mind is distraught. You shall have time to think this over; but remember, Kate, we must fight fire with fire, and the time has come when you must choose between us."

And then, very wisely, he slipped from the room.

CHAPTER 26

ON THE promenade outside he met Sloan, the wireless operator, on his way to Captain Henshaw's cabin with a slip of paper in his hand. Sloan winked at him broadly.

"The good news has come, sir," he grinned. "Take a look at this!"

And McTee eagerly read the typewritten slip.

Beatrice is rallying. Doctors have decided effusion of blood was not hemorrhage. Opinion now very hopeful.

"Will that bring the old boy around for a while?" asked Sloan.

"He'll slip you a twenty on the strength of that and give you a drink as well," said McTee.

They reached the cabin and entered together to find that White Henshaw lay on the couch in the corner. His physical strength was apparently exhausted, and one long, lean arm dangled to the floor. At sight of the dreaded wireless operator with the message in his hand, his yellow face turned from yellow to pale ivory. He rose and supported himself with one hand against the wall, scowling as if he dared them to notice his weakness.

"Good news!" called Sloan cheerily, and extended the paper.

The captain snatched the paper, his eyes were positively wolfish while he devoured the message.

"Sloan—good lad," he stammered. "Stay by your instrument every minute, my boy. Before night we'll have word that she's past all danger."

Sloan touched his cap and withdrew.

"Good news!" said McTee amiably. "I'm mighty glad to hear it, captain."

The old man fell back into a chair, holding the precious piece of paper with its written lie in both trembling hands.

"Good news," he croaked. "Aye, McTee. You were right, lad! Those damned doctors don't know their business. They're making the case out bad so they'll get more credit for the cure. See how they're fooling with me— and me with my heart on fire in the middle of the sea!"

His eyes wandered strangely in the midst of his exultation.

"That would be a strange death, eh, McTee—to burn in the middle of the sea with a ship full of gold?"

The Scotchman shuddered.

"Forget that, man. You're not going to burn at sea. You're going to reach port with all your gold and you're going to stand beside Beatrice and say—"

Henshaw broke in: "And say, 'Beatrice, I've come to make you happy. We'll leave this country where the fogs are so thick and the sun never shines, and we'll go south, far south, where there's summer all the year.' That's what I'll say!"

"Right," nodded McTee. "If her lungs are weak, that's the place to take her."

Henshaw jerked erect in his chair. "Weak lungs? Who said she had weak lungs? McTee, you're a fool! A little cold on the chest, that's all that's the matter with the girl! The doctors have made the sickness— they and their rotten medicines! And now they're making sport out of White Henshaw. I'll skin them alive, I will!"

McTee lighted a cigar and nodded judiciously as he puffed it.

"Very good idea, Henshaw. If you want me to, I'll go along and help you out."

"You're a brick, McTee. Maybe I'll need you. Getting old; not what I used to be."

"I see you're not," said McTee boldly.

Henshaw scowled: "What do you mean?"

"That affair of Harrigan. He's still going scot-free, you know."

"Right! McTee, I'm getting feeble-minded, but I'll make up for lost time."

He caught up pen and paper, while McTee drew a long breath of relief. A moment later he was astonished to note that the captain had not written a single letter.

"I'd forgotten," murmured Henshaw. "When I started to write that order this morning—just as I was putting pen to paper—in came Sloan with the message from the doctors saying that Beatrice was in a critical situation. It may be, captain, that this message is bad luck for me, eh?"

"Nonsense," said McTee easily, gripping his hand with rage, while he fought to control his voice. "You mustn't let superstitions run away with you."

"So! So!" frowned Henshaw. "You're a young man to give me advice, McTee. I've followed superstitions all my life. I tell you there's something in those stargazing devils of the South Seas. They know things that aren't in the books."

"What about the old fool who prophesied that you'd die by fire at sea?"

Henshaw shivered, and his eyes narrowed as he stared at McTee.

"How do you know he's an old fool, eh? We haven't reached port yet—not by a long sight!"

"Well," said McTee, with a carefully assumed carelessness, "this ship belongs to you—you're the skipper; but on a boat I was captain of, no damned engineer would pull my beard and tell me to rightabout. They never got away with a line of chatter like that when Black McTee was speaking to them. Never!"

At this comparison the face of Henshaw grew marvelously evil.

"McTee," he said, "men step lively when you speak to them—but they jump out of their skins when they hear White Henshaw's voice."

"That's what I've heard," said the other dauntlessly, "but d'you think Campbell ever would have taken this chance if he didn't know you're not what you used to be?"

For reply Henshaw set his teeth and dipped the pen into the ink. As he poised it above the paper, Sloan appeared at the door calling: "One minute, captain!"

The captain turned livid and rose slowly, crumpling the paper as he did so and letting it drop to the floor.

"Out with it!" he muttered in a hoarse whisper. "She's worse again! Damn you, McTee, I told you this message was bad luck!"

The wireless operator was much puzzled and glance from the Scotchman to his skipper.

"I only wanted to know, sir, if you wish to send an answer to this last wireless. Any congratulations?"

"No—get out!"

And as Sloan fled from the door with a wondering side glance at McTee, Henshaw sank back into his chair, picked up the paper on which he was about to write, and tore it into small bits. Not until this task was finished was he able to speak to McTee.

"D'you see now? Is there nothing in my superstitions? Why, sir, just holding that pen over this piece of damnable paper brought Sloan on the run to my door. If I'd written a single word, he'd of had a message from the doctors saying that Beatrice was dying. I know!"

"You really think," began McTee, and some of his furious impatience crept into his voice—"you really think that writing on that piece of paper with your pen would have brought in Sloan with a wireless message from the mainland?"

Henshaw shook his head slowly.

"There's no use trying to explain these things," he said, "but sometimes, McTee, there's a small voice that comes up inside of me and tells me what to do and what not to do. When I first saw the picture of Beatrice—that one where she's just a slip of a child—there was a voice that said: 'Here's the spirit of your dead wife come back to life. You must work for her and cherish her.' So I've done it. And because I started to do it, the voice never left me. It warned me when to put to sea and when to stay hi port. It gave me a hint when to buy and when to sell, and the result is that I'm rich—rich—rich. Gold in my hand and gold in my brain, McTee!"

The Scotchman began to feel more and more that old age or his monomania had shaken White Henshaw's reason, but he said bitterly: "And I suppose, if that voice never fails you and if these South Seas natives can read the future, that you are bound to burn at sea?"

"Damn you!" said Henshaw, terribly moved. "What devil keeps putting that in your brain? Isn't it in mine all the day and all the night? Don't I see hellfire in the dark? Don't I see the same flames, blue and thin, dancing in the light of the sun at midday? Is the thing ever out of my mind? Were you put on this ship to keep dinning the idea into my ears? If there's something more than the life on earth, then there must be a hell—and if there's a hell, then it's real hellfire that I see!"

He paused and pointed a gaunt, trembling arm at McTee:

"D'you understand? The men I've killed before they died—they send their spirits here to walk beside me. They wait in the dark—and they whisper in my ear!"

McTee swallowed hard and commenced to edge toward the door.

"Farley is always hanging around—Farley, as I saw him on the beach that last time in his loincloth, with his pig eyes; sometimes he seems to be begging me to take pity on him; sometimes he seems to be laughing at me. And he's always got his hand outstretched. And Collins comes stroking his beard in the way he had, and he keeps his hand stretched out to me. What do they want? Alms! Alms! Alms! They want my soul for alms to take it below and burn it in the hellfire—the thin, blue flames!"

He stopped in the midst of his ravings and drew himself erect, a smile of infinite cruelty on his lips.

"Let them all come with their damned, empty palms! They're ghosts, and they cannot stop me so long as I follow the small voice that's inside of me. They can't stop me, and I'll win back to Beatrice. There I'm safe—safe! Her hands are thin and light and cool and as fragrant as flowers. She'll lay them on my eyelids and I'll go to sleep! And the ghosts will close their empty hands. Ha! McTee, d'you know aught of the power of a woman's love?"

He stepped close to the burly Scotchman.

"Keep off," growled McTee. "I want none of you! There's poison in your touch!"

He raised his hand like a guard, but two lean, thin hands, incredibly strong, closed on his wrists.

"A woman's love," went on the old buccaneer of the South Seas, "is stronger than armor plate to save the man she cares for. You can't see it; you could never see it! But I tell you there are times when the ghosts have come close to me, and then sometimes I've seen the shadows of thin, small hands come in front of me and push them back. The hands of Beatrice push them back, and they're helpless to harm me!"

CHAPTER 27

BUT MCTEE wrenched his arms away and fled out on the deck. He blundered into Jerry Hovey, who started back at sight of him.

"What's happened, sir?" asked the bos'n. "Been seein' ghosts?"

"Damn you," growled McTee, "I had a nap and a bad dream—a hell of a nightmare."

"You look it! You heard what Harrigan said? Does that sound as if I had enough backing?"

"If the rest of them are as strong for it as Harrigan, it does."

"As strong for it as Harrigan? Between you and me—just a whisper in your ear—I don't think Harrigan is half as strong for it as he talks. I don't trust him, somehow."

"No?"

"Look here," said the bos'n cautiously. "We hear there was once some trouble between you and Harrigan?"

"Well?"

"Would you waste much tune if somethin' was to happen to him—say in the middle of the night, silent and unexpected?"

"I would not! Take him by the foot and heave him into the sea. Very good idea, Hovey. Is he getting the eyes of the lads too much?"

Hovey fenced: "He's a landlubber, and he don't understand sea things. He's better out of the way."

"How'll you do it?" asked McTee softly. "Speak out, Hovey. Would you try your own hand on Harrigan?"

"Not me! I know a better way. There's one that's in the mutiny who has a hand as strong as mine—almost—and a foot as silent as the paw of a cat. I'll give him the tip."

"And now for the details of the attack," said McTee, anxious not to lay too much stress upon the destruction of Harrigan.

"Here it is," answered Hovey, and entered into an elaborate description of all their plans. McTee listened with faraway eyes. He heard the words, but he was thinking of the death of Harrigan.

That invincible Irishman, after his talk with Hovey in front of the cabin of Kate, returned to the cool room of the chief engineer. The worthy Campbell, in wait for the ultimatum of White Henshaw, had been fortifying himself steadily with liquor, and by the middle of the afternoon he had reached a state in which he had no care for consequences; he would have defied all the powers upon earth and beyond it.

The next morning, as he went up to his usual task of scrubbing the bridge, Harrigan thought he perceived a possible reason why his persecution was being neglected. It was the picture of McTee and Kate Malone leaning at the rail. McTee was content. There was no doubt of that. He leaned above Kate and talked seriously down into her face. Harrigan was mightily tempted to turn about and climb to the bridge from the other side of the deck, but he made himself march on and begin whistling a tune.

McTee raised his head instantly, and, staring at the Irishman, he murmured a word to Kate, and she turned and regarded Harrigan with an almost painful curiosity. He was about to swagger past her when she shook off the detaining hand of McTee and ran to the Irishman.

"Dan," she said eagerly, and laid a hand on his arm.

"Come back, Kate," growled McTee. "You've promised me not to speak—"

"Did you promise him not to speak with me again?" broke in Harrigan.

"I only meant—" she began.

"It's little I care what you meant," said the Irishman coldly, and he shook off her hand. "Go play with McTee. I want none of ye! After I've slaved for ye an' saved ye from God knows what, ye dare to turn and make them eyes cold and distant when ye look at me? Ah-h, get back to McTee! I'm through with ye!"

She only insisted the more: "I *will* speak to you, Dan!"

"Come away, Kate," urged McTee, grinding his teeth. "Doesn't this prove what I told you?"

"I don't care what it proves," she said hotly. "Dan, I've been thinking grisly things of you. I simply can't believe them now that I look you in the face."

"Whisht!" said Harrigan, and his face was black. "Have you the right to doubt me?"

She answered sadly: "I have, Dan."

The Irishman turned slowly away and started up for the bridge without answer. As he went, he groaned beneath his breath: "Ochone! Ochone! She's heard!"

He could not dream how she knew of the mutiny, but if it was carried through, he was damned in her eyes forever. What she guessed McTee must know. What McTee knew must be familiar to White Henshaw, yet Henshaw could not know, for if he did, the ringleaders would be instantly clapped into irons. Once or twice he looked down from his work to Kate and McTee. They still leaned at the rail, talking seriously.

And McTee was saying: "I have learned what I want to know. Every detail of the plot is in my hands. Now I am going to the cabin of White Henshaw and tell him everything. It's the simplest way. And you've started a suspicion in the mind of Harrigan. He'll spread the word to the rest of the mutineers, and they'll be on their watch against us."

She made a little gesture of appeal. "I couldn't help speaking to him, Angus. Suspecting him of such a thing is like—is like suspecting myself!"

"Let it go. It's done. Now I'm going up to see White Henshaw. The old man will be crazy when he hears it."

He found the captain giving some orders to Salvain, and waited until they were alone. Then he said: "There are about ten of us against the rest of the crew of the ship. Can we hold them in case of a mutiny?"

He had planned this laconic statement carefully, expecting to see Henshaw turn pale and stammer in terror. Instead, the captain regarded McTee with quietly contemplative eyes.

"So," he murmured, "you've heard of the mutiny?"

The tables were completely turned on the Scotchman. He gasped: "You have known all the time?"

"Certainly," said Henshaw; "I even know every word that Hovey said to you."

McTee turned crimson.

"I have eyes that see everything on the ship," went on Henshaw, as if he wished to cover the embarrassment of the Scotchman, "and I have ears which hear everything. I have lines of information tangled through the forecastle. I can almost guess what they are about to think, let alone what they will speak or do. The blockheads are always planning a mutiny, though I confess none of them have ever taken the proportions of this one. However, this will go the way of the rest."

"The way of the rest?" queried McTee almost stupidly.

"Yes. They plan to hold their action till we're close to the land. About that time I'll call up one or two of the ring-leaders and tell them just what they have planned to do. That'll make them think I have unknown means of meeting the mutiny. It will die."

McTee sat down, loosened his shirt at the throat, and gaped upon Henshaw as a child might gape upon a magician.

"I don't blame you for taking a day to think over the temptation," smiled the old buccaneer. "The gold I showed you would have tempted any man. But I'm glad you came to me. I expected you last night. It took you a little longer to settle the details in your mind, eh?"

"Henshaw, I feel like a yellow dog!"

"Come! Come! You're a man after my own heart. You took the temptation in your hand—you looked it over—and then you turned away from it. Well, and suppose the mutiny should actually come to the breaking point; they would be right in thinking I have means of fighting them. I have no firearms on the ship; they know that. They don't know that I have these."

He went into the next room and returned carrying a heavy box. This he placed on the desk and took a small, heavy ball of metal from it.

"A bomb?" queried McTee.

"It is. The moment a group gathers, one of these tossed among them will end the mutiny the moment it begins."

McTee handed back the bomb in silence. There was something about this cold-blooded way of speaking of death which was not cruelty—it was something greater—it was an absolute disregard of life.

"Of course," said Henshaw, as he came back from depositing the box in the next room, "there are only half a dozen of those bombs, but that will be enough. The explosion of a couple of them would just about wreck the deck. However, the mutiny will never reach the point of action. I'll see to that. What always ties the hands of the crew is that it lacks real leaders. Hovey, for instance, will turn to water when I say three words about the mutiny to him."

"But Harrigan," said McTee quietly, "will not."

"The Irishman!" Henshaw muttered. "I forgot. McTee, I'm getting old!"

"Only careless," answered the other, "but it's a bad thing to be careless where Harrigan is concerned. A man like that, Henshaw, could lead your mutineers, and lead them well. Hovey told me that every one of the crew looks up to the Irishman."

"He's got to be crippled—or put out of the way," stated Henshaw calmly. "I was a fool. I forgot about Harrigan."

"It may be," said McTee, "that he'll be put out of the way tonight."

"McTee, I begin to see that you have brains."

The latter waved the sinister compliment aside.

"Suppose the little—er—experiment fails? Doesn't it occur to you that that message might be written out and sent to Campbell?"

The captain changed color, and his eyes shifted.

"I've told you—" he began.

"Nonsense," said McTee. "I'll write the thing, if you want, and all you'll have to do is to sign it."

"Would that make any difference?" asked Henshaw wistfully.

"Of course," said McTee. "Here we go. You've got to do something to tame Harrigan, captain, or there'll be the deuce to pay."

And as he spoke, he picked up pen and paper and began to write, Henshaw in the meantime walking to the door in an agony of apprehension as if he expected to see the dreaded figure of Sloan appear. McTee wrote:

From Captain Henshaw to Chief Engineer Douglas Campbell

Sir:

On the receipt of this order, you will at once place Daniel Harrigan at work passing coal, beginning this day with a double shift, and continuing hereafter one shift a day.

(Signed)

"Here you are, captain," he called, and Henshaw turned reluctantly from the door and sat down at the table.

"Bad luck's in it," he muttered, "but something has to be done— something has to be done!"

He wrote: "Captain Hensh—" but at this point the voice of Sloan spoke from the open door.

"A message, captain."

With a choked cry Henshaw whirled and rose, supporting himself against the edge of the table with both trembling hands. His accusing eyes were on McTee.

"Sloan!" he called in his hoarse whisper at last, but still his damning gaze held hard upon McTee.

The wireless operator advanced a step at a time into the room, placed the written message on the edge of the table, and then sprang back as if in mortal fear. Henshaw, still keeping his glance upon the Scotchman with a terrible earnestness, picked up the sheet of paper on which he had been signing his name, and tore it slowly, methodically, into small strips. As the last of the small fragments fluttered to the floor, his hand went out to the message Sloan had brought and drew it to his side. He waved his arm in a sweeping gesture that commanded the other two from his presence, and they slipped from the cabin without a word.

CHAPTER 28

"SHE'S DEAD?" McTee asked softly when they stood on the promenade outside.

"She is. She must have been dying at about the time I brought in that other message—the one you told me to bring."

They avoided each other's eyes. Inside the cabin they heard a faint sound like paper crumpled up. Then they caught a moan from the room—a soft sound such as the wind makes when it hums around the corners of a tall building.

They were silent for a time, listening with painful intentness. Not another murmur came from the cabin. Sloan wiped his wet forehead and whispered shakily: "I wouldn't mind it so much if he'd curse and rave. But to sit like that, not making a sound—it ain't natural, Captain McTee."

"Hush, you fool," said McTee. "White Henshaw is alone with his dead. And it's me that he blames for it. I brought him the bad luck."

Sloan shuddered.

"Then I wouldn't have your name for ten thousand dollars, sir."

"If there's bad luck," said McTee solemnly, for every sailor has some superstitious belief, "it's on the entire ship—on one of the crew as well as on me. We'll have to pay for this—all of us—and pay high. We're apt to *feel* it before long. And I've got to go back to that cabin after a while!"

He spoke it as another man might say: "And an hour from now I have to face the firing squad."

But when he returned to the cabin, he heard no outburst of reproaches from White Henshaw. The door to Henshaw's bedroom was closed, and McTee could hear the captain stirring about in it, working at some nameless task over which he hummed continually, now and then breaking into little snatches of song. McTee was stupefied. He tried to explain to himself by imagining that Henshaw was one of those hard-headed men who live for the present and never waste time thinking of the past. He had made many plans for his granddaughter. Now she was dead, and he dismissed her from his mind.

This explanation might be the truth, but nevertheless the steady humming wore on McTee's nerves until finally he knocked on the door of the inner cabin. It was dusk by this time, and when Henshaw opened the door, he was carrying a lantern.

"You!" he muttered. "Well, captain?"

"You seem busy," said McTee uneasily, shifting under the steady light from the lantern. "I thought I might be able to help you."

"At the work I'm doing no man can help," answered Henshaw.

"What work?"

"I'm calculating profit and loss."

"On your cargo?"

"Cargo? Yes, yes! Profit and loss on this cargo."

And he broke into a harsh laugh. Obviously Henshaw was lying, yet the Scotchman went on with the conversation, eager to draw out some hidden meaning.

"It's an odd idea of yours, this, to bring a shipment of wheat from the south seas to Central America."

"Aye, the first time it's ever been done. This wheat came all the way from Australia and the United States, and now it's going back again. I'll tell you why. Wheat is scarce for export even in the States just now, so I'm taking a gambling chance on getting this to port before the first quantities come from the north. If I get in in time, I'll clean up—big."

"I understand," said McTee.

The captain raised his lantern again and shone it in the eyes of McTee.

"Do you understand?" he queried. "Do you?"

And he broke again into the harsh laughter. McTee started back with a scowl.

"What's the mystery, captain? What's the secret you're laughing about?"

Again Henshaw chuckled.

"You're a curious man, McTee. Well, well! What am I laughing about? Money always makes me want to laugh, and now I'm laughing about money. Do you understand that? No, you don't. Perhaps you will before long. Patience, my friend!"

For some reason the blood of McTee grew cold and colder as he listened. His original suspicion of insanity grew weaker. He was being mocked, and the mad do not mock.

"So tonight is the last night of Harrigan, eh?" said Henshaw suddenly.

"In the name of God," said McTee, deeply shaken, "why do you speak of that? Yes, tonight he dies!"

"Alone!" said Henshaw in a changed voice. "He dies alone! It must be a grim thing to die alone at sea—to slip into the black water—to drink the salt—a little struggle—and then the light goes out. So!"

He shivered and folded his arms. He seemed to be embracing himself to find warmth.

"But to die in the middle of the ocean with many men around you," he went on, speaking half to himself, "that would not be so bad. What do you say, McTee?"

But McTee was not in a mood for speaking. He only stared, fascinated and dumb. Henshaw continued: "In the middle of night, with the engines thrumming, and the lights burning in every port, suppose a ship should put her nose under the surface and dive for the bottom! The men are singing in the forecastle, and suddenly their song goes out. The captain is in the wheelhouse. He is dreaming of his home town, maybe, when he sees the black waters rising over the prow. He thinks it is a dream and rubs his eyes. Before he can look again, the waves are upon him. There is no alarm; the wireless, perhaps, is broken; the boats, perhaps, are useless; and so the brave ship dives down to Davy Jones's locker with all on board, and the next minute the waves wash over the spot and rub out all memory of those who died there. Well, well, McTee, there's a way of dying that would please White Henshaw more than a death in a bed at a home port, with the landsharks sitting round your bed grinning and nodding out your minutes of life. Ha?"

But Black McTee, like a frightened child caught in a dark room, turned and fled in shameless fear into the deep night. Not till he was far aft did he stop in a quiet place to think of Harrigan dying alone, choking in the black water.

But Harrigan was far from fear. He lay on the deck above the forecastle, cradled by the swing of the bows. He shook away the lurking horror of the mutiny and gave himself up to peace.

In the midst of his sleep he dreamed of lying in a pitch-dark room and staring up at a brilliant point of light, like a dark lantern partially unshuttered. And suddenly Harrigan woke, and looking up, he caught a flashing point of light directly above his eyes. In another moment he was aware of the dark figure of a man crouched beside him, and then he knew that the light which glittered over his head was the shimmer of the stars against a steel blade.

The knife, as he stared, jerked up and then down with a sweep; Harrigan shot up his hand to meet the blow, and his grip fastened on a wrist. Wrenching on that wrist, he jerked himself to his knees, and the knife clattered on the deck, but at the same instant the other man—a dim figure which he could barely make out in the thick night—rushed on him, a shoulder struck against his chest, and he was thrown sprawling on the deck, sliding with the toss of the deck underneath the rail. He would have fallen overboard had he not kept his grip on that wrist, and as he reached the perilous edge, the other man jerked back to free his arm.

He succeeded, but the effort checked the slide of Harrigan's great body, and the next instant the Irishman was on his feet. He drove at the elusive figure with his balled fist, but the other ducked beneath the blow and fled down the ladder. Harrigan stopped only long enough to sweep up the fallen knife before he followed, but when he reached the edge of the deck, the waist of the ship extending back to the main cabin was empty. The man, whoever he was, must have fled into the forecastle.

Harrigan knew that if one of the sailors had dared to attack him, he must be suspected, and if he was suspected by one, that one would poison the minds of a dozen others in a short time. It was even possible that someone in authority had given orders for his death. With this in mind he climbed down the ladder and opened the door of the forecastle. He found the sailors sitting in a loose circle on the floor rolling battered dice out of a time-blackened leather box.

Harrigan sat down on the edge of his bunk, produced the captured knife, and commenced to sharpen it slowly, without ostentation, on the sole of his shoe. It was already of a razor keenness. It was a carving knife evidently stolen from the galley of the ship; it had been ground so often that the steel which remained was thin and narrow. A sharp blow with that knife would drive it to the handle through human flesh. As he passed it slowly back and forth across his shoe, Harrigan watched the faces of the others with a side glance.

One or two looked up frankly and nodded approval when they saw his occupation. The others, however, kept at their game, and of these the only one to pay no attention to his presence was Jerry Hovey. It convinced Harrigan at once that the bos'n had given orders for his death. It might have been the bos'n himself who had made the attempt just a moment before and had retreated to the forecastle.

On the other hand, the bos'n seemed to be breathing regularly, and the man with whom he had fought would not be able to keep his chest from heaving a little after that violent effort. It was more probable that one of the men who lay in their bunks had made the attempt, but it would be useless to examine them. Then his glance fell on Kamasura, the cabin boy.

The little, flat-faced Jap was a favorite with Jerry Hovey, and he was permitted to come forward whenever he pleased to the forecastle. He now sat on a box against a wall, watching the dice game with his slant eyes. Once or twice he met the searching scrutiny of Harrigan with a calm glance, and when it was repeated for the third time, nodded and grinned in the most friendly manner.

Harrigan was about to dismiss his suspicion from his mind, when he noticed that the Jap's arms were folded and the hands thrust up the opposite sleeves, concealing both wrists. Harrigan considered a moment, and then stooped over and commenced to unlace his boots. When the first one was unloosened, he kicked it off, but with such careless vigor that it skidded far across the floor and smashed against the box on which Kamasura sat. The little Oriental leaped to his feet and caught up the shoe. As he did so, Harrigan's watchful eye saw a bright-red spot on the Jap's wrist. That was where the grip of his fingers had lain when they struggled on the deck above.

"'Scuse me, Kamasura," he called cheerily, and raised his hand to betoken that the boot had come from him.

There was a flash of teeth and a glint of almond eyes as the Jap grinned in answer and the boot was tossed back. Harrigan caught it, but his eye was not on the shoe. He was staring covertly at Jerry Hovey, and now he saw the gray-blue eyes of the bos'n flash up and glance with a singular meaning at Kamasura. If he had heard every detail of the plot, Harrigan could not have understood more fully. Thereafter, every moment he spent on the *Heron* would be full of danger, but apparently Hovey had confided his hatred of the Irishman to Kamasura alone. If Hovey had spoken to the rest of the forecastle, those blunt sailors would have showed their feelings by some scowling side glance at Harrigan. It flashed across his mind that the reason Hovey wished him out of the way was because he feared him.

CHAPTER 29

HE SLIPPED onto his bunk and lay with his hands folded under his head, thinking; for between the danger from the leader of the mutiny and the danger from McTee and Henshaw, he was utterly confused. He made out the voices of the two gamblers, Hall and Cochrane.

"Three deuces to beat," said Hall.

"I'd beat three fives to get Van Roos," answered Cochrane.

Jan Van Roos was the second mate, a genial Dutchman with rosy cheeks and a hearty laugh for all occasions; but he was an excellent sailor and a strict disciplinarian. Therefore he had won the hatred of the crew. The entire group of mutineers had shaken dice to have the disposing of the mate in case he was captured alive. Now the dice rattled and clicked on the deck as Cochrane made his cast.

"Forty-three!" called Cochrane. "Now watch the fours."

He swept up the other three dice and made his second cast. Another four rolled upon the deck. He had won Van Roos, to dispose of him as he saw fit. Harrigan heard the rumble of Sam Hall's cursing.

"Easy, lad," said Cochrane soothingly. "We'll work on Van Roos together, and if we don't sweat every ounce of blubber out of his fat carcass, my name is not Garry."

There was a sharp knock at the door of the forecastle, and a moment later Shida, the other Japanese cabin boy, entered and came directly to the bunk of Harrigan.

He whispered in the ear of the Irishman: "Meester Harrigan, get up. Cap'n McTee, he want."

"Where is he?" growled Harrigan.

"I show."

Harrigan slipped on his shoes and followed Shida aft, wondering. The little, quick-footed Jap brought him back of the wheelhouse and then disappeared. Leaning against the rail was McTee, unaware of their coming and peering out at the wake of the ship.

As the Heron's stern dipped to a trough of a wave that towered blackly into the night, the outlines of McTee's form were blurred, but the next moment he was tossed up against the very heart of the starry sky. With that peculiar mixture of fear and thrilling exultation which he always felt when he came into the presence of the captain, Harrigan drew close. Perhaps the sailor had chosen this heaving afterdeck as the place for their final death struggle, ending when one of them was hurled into the black ocean.

It was this thought which gave the ring to his voice when he called, "I've come, McTee!"

The captain whirled, bracing himself against the rail with both hands, as though prepared to meet an attempt to thrust him overboard. Then— and Harrigan thought his ears deceived him as he listened—McTee said with a great, outgoing breath: "Thank God!"

He explained: "Come closer; talk soft! Harrigan, guard yourself tonight. There'll be an attempt at your life!"

"Another?" queried Harrigan.

"They've tackled you already?"

Harrigan took out the knife and waved it in the faint starlight.

"They did," he said jauntily, "and they left this behind them as a token."

"Listen," said McTee; "it's not for nothing that men call me Black, but all evening I've been remembering the time when we took hands in the trough of the sea. I've thought of that, Harrigan, and it made me weak inside—"

He paused, but Harrigan would not speak.

"Because I planned your death tonight, Dan."

"Angus, the steel ain't been sharpened that can kill me."

"Don't be too confident. Get every word I say. I'm washing my soul out for you. It's Hovey and the little Jap, Kamasura, that you'll have to guard against."

"I know 'em both."

"D'you mean to say—"

"No, I didn't make 'em confess, but I saw 'em lookin' at each other. What made you hitch up with swine like them? Was it because of—her?"

"Yes."

"Then I forgive you for it. Angus, I got a sort of a desire to shake hands with you. There's nothin' but swine an' snakes aboard the Heron. I'd like to feel the grip of a man's hand."

They fumbled in the dark and then their hands met. They retained that grasp till the ship sank twice to the deep shadow of the trough and swung up again to the crest.

"There's no peace between us till she's out of the way," muttered Harrigan at last. "What d'you say, Angus?"

"Harrigan, there are times when you're a poet. Strip!"

The Irishman was tearing off his shirt, when three crashing, rattling explosions sent a shudder through the Heron, and his arms dropped nervelessly.

"Where was it?" gasped Harrigan.

"Forward," answered McTee.

"Kate!" they cried in the same breath, and rushed for the main cabin.

CHAPTER 30

THE DECKS were already thick with half-dressed sailors. Here and there lanterns gleamed, and what they showed was the three lifeboats of the Heron—two on one side of the cabin and one on the other—blown into matchwood. Only shapeless fragments and bundles of kindling wood dangled from the davits.

Captain Henshaw, cool and calm in his white clothes, stood with folded arms examining the wreckage on one side.

The sailors from the forecastle went here and there, muttering, growling surlily; for a shrewd blow had been struck at their plan of mutiny, the last item of which was to abandon the Heron off a deserted coast and then row ashore in the lifeboats. Over their clamor and cursing broke two voices, one accusing in a deep bass and the other protesting innocence in a harsh treble. It was the third mate, Eric Borgson, who approached carrying little Kamasura under his arm like a bundle.

"Here's the little devil who done the work," he snarled, and flung Kamasura at the feet of White Henshaw.

The Japanese are a brave people, but in that dreadful presence Kamasura made no effort to regain his feet, but remained on his knees, groveling and clinging to the hands of the captain, while he shrieked out an explanation. To remove his hands from those clinging fingers, Henshaw simply raised his foot, laid it against the breast of the Jap, and thrust out. The kick sent Kamasura rolling head over heels till he crashed against the rail. He lay partially stunned by the impact, and Eric Borgson, bellowing his enjoyment of this pleasant jest, collared poor Kamasura and dragged him back before White Henshaw. The Jap was now inarticulate with terror and pain.

"I was comin' down out of the wheelhouse," said the mate, "to get a bite of lunch—this bein' a night watch—when I seen this little yellow rat sneakin' down the deck like a thief. I didn't think nothin' much about it, supposin' he'd just lifted some chow, maybe, and then I heard them explosions. They knocked me off my pins, but I scrambled over an' collared this fellow. He showed he was guilty right off the bat by yellin' for mercy."

"Captain, captain!" screamed Kamasura. "Lies, lies-all lies. I go down the deck—"

The heavy hand of Eric Borgson smashed against Kamasura's mouth. The Jap sagged back, was jerked upright, and the mate's clubbed fist jarred home again.

"Lies, are they?" thundered Borgson. "I'll teach you to say that word to Eric Borgson, ha!"

And he struck the half-conscious Jap again full in the face. There was a slight commotion in the back of the gathering crowd of sailors. Harrigan was urging forward, but he was caught by the iron hands of McTee and held back.

"For the love of Mike," moaned the Irishman softly, "let me at that swine of a mate!"

"Shut up!" cautioned McTee savagely, but in a whisper. "That's the Jap who tried to knife you!"

"I will—I'll shut up," sighed Harrigan, panting, "but ah-h, to get in punchin' distance of Borgson for one second!"

"What shall we do with him?" Borgson was asking.

"Captain!" begged the husky voice of Kamasura, fighting his way back to semi-consciousness.

"If he tries to speak again, smash his mouth in," said Henshaw without raising his voice. "Tonight put him in irons. I'll tend to him tomorrow. Go get the irons. Hovey, take Kamasura below."

"Aye, aye, sir," said Hovey, and caught the Jap by the arms behind.

That touch quieted Kamasura, and as he was led off, he began to whisper quickly.

The moment they were away from the crowd, Hovey said: "Say it slow—no, you don't have to beg me to help you. I'll do what I can. You know that. Now tell me what you saw."

"Cap'n McTee—behind the wireless house—holding the hand of Harrigan. They were talkin' soft—like friends!"

"By God," muttered Hovey fiercely, "an' yet McTee told me he wanted Harrigan put out of the way. He's double-crossin' us. They're teamin' it together. What did they say?"

The Jap spat blood copiously before he could answer: "I could not hear."

"You ain't worth your salt," responded Hovey.

"I cannot help—I am crush—I am defeat. Do not let them bring me before Henshaw. To look at him—it puts the cold in my heart. I cannot speak. I shall die—I—"

"Keep your head up," said Hovey. "There's nothing I can say that'll help you—just now. Later on you'll be able to deal with Henshaw and Borgson just the way they dealt with you. Does that help any?"

"Ah-h," whispered the Jap and drew in his breath sharply with delight.

"I might start the boys—I might turn them loose on the ship," went on Hovey, "but the time ain't come yet for that. We're too far from the coast. Whatever happens, Kamasura, can you promise me to keep your face shut about the mutiny?"

"Yes-s."

"Even if they was to tie you up an' feed you the lash? Henshaw's equal to that."

Kamasura stammered, hesitated.

"Don't make no mistake," said Hovey fiercely, "because we'll be standin' close, some of us, an' the first tune you open your damned mouth, we'll bash your head in. Get me?"

The entrance of Eric Borgson made it impossible for the Jap to answer with words, but his eyes were eloquent with promise. Hovey started back for the forecastle; he had much to say to the sailors, and thereafter life on the Heron would be equally dangerous for both Harrigan and McTee.

The two, in the meantime, were making their way aft shoulder to shoulder. When they reached the stretch of deck behind the wireless house, McTee said: "Harrigan, what's it to be? Are you for fighting it out?"

"I'm with you in anything you say," retorted the dauntless Irishman, and then with a changed voice, "but I'm feelin' sort of sick inside, Angus. Did ye see that murtherin' dog smash the mouth of that Jap when he hadn't the strength to lift his head? Ah-h!"

"I'm sick, too," said McTee, "but not because of the Jap. It's something worse that bothers me."

"What?"

"It's the thought of White Henshaw, Dan. The brain of that old devil is going back on him. I think he loves death more than life. His memories of what he's done put him in hell every minute he lives."

"Go easy, McTee," said Harrigan. "D'you mean to say that Henshaw blew up those boats—an' his ship still in the middle of the Pacific?"

"I say nothing. All I know is that he talked damned queerly of how wonderful it would be if a ship in the middle of the sea put her nose under the waves and started for Davy Jones's locker. Yes, if she went down with all hands—dived for the bottom, in fact."

"What can we do?"

"I don't know, but I'm beginning to think that this ship—and our lives— would be safer in the hands of Hovey and his gang of cutthroats than they will be under White Henshaw. Queer things are going to happen on the *Heron*, Harrigan, mark my word."

"You think Henshaw blew up the boats so not one of the crew could escape?"

"It sounds too crazy to repeat."

"McTee!"

"Yes, I'm thinking of her, too."

"Between the mutiny and the crazy captain, Angus, it'll take both of us to pull her through."

"It will."

"Then gimme your hand once more, cap'n. We're in the trough of the sea once more, an' God knows when we'll reach dry land, but while we're on the *Heron*, we're brothers once more. For her sake I'll forget I hate you till we've got the honest ground under our feet once more."

"When the time comes," said McTee, "it'll be a wonderful fight."

"It will," agreed Harrigan fervently. "But first, McTee, we must let her know that we're standin' shoulder to shoulder to fight for her. Otherwise she won't give us her trust."

"You're right again. We'll go to her cabin now and tell her. But don't give her a hint of all that we fear. She already knows about the mutiny—and she knows about your part in it."

"You saw to that, McTee?" said Harrigan softly, as he pulled on his shirt.

"I did."

"Ah-h, Angus, that fight'll be even better than I was afther thinkin'."

And they went forward, walking again shoulder to shoulder. It was Harrigan who stood in front at her door and knocked. She opened it wide, but at sight of him started to slam it again. He blocked it with his foot.

"I've not come for my own sake," he said in a hard voice, "but the two of us have come together."

MAX BRAND

He jerked his thumb over his shoulder, and she made out the towering form of McTee. At that she opened the door, glancing curiously from one to the other. The eyes of Harrigan went from her face to McTee, and his eyes flamed.

"Speak up, McTee," he said savagely. "Tell her you lied about me."

The Scotchman glowered upon him.

"I'll tell her what I've just found out," he answered coldly, and turned to Kate. "We were mistaken in what we thought when we overheard Hovey talking with Harrigan. Dan was simply playing a part with them— he was trying to learn their plans so as to use them against the mutineers when the time came."

There was a joyousness in her voice that cut McTee like a knife as she cried: "I knew! I knew! My instinct fought for you, Dan. I couldn't believe what I heard!"

"What you both heard?" he said bitterly. "I remember now. It was when I talked with Hovey in front of this cabin?"

"Ask no more questions," said McTee. "I'm seeing red now."

"Black! You see nothin' but black, ye swine! The soot in your soul is a stain hi your eyes, McTee."

They turned toward the door, but she sprang before it and set her shoulders against the boards.

"Sit down—you too, Dan."

They obeyed slowly, McTee taking the edge of the bunk and Harrigan lowering his bulk to the little campstool, which groaned beneath his weight. She sat on a chair between them, while she looked from face to face.

"When you came in you were friends," she said, "and the only thing that could bring you to friendship was danger. There is danger. What?"

They exchanged glances of wonder at this shrewd interpretation.

"There is danger," said McTee at length, "and it's a danger which is something more than the mutiny, perhaps."

"I will tell it," said Harrigan.

He drew his chair closer to Kate and leaned over so that his face was near hers. She knew at once that he had forgotten all about the presence of McTee.

"Kate, I will not lie to ye, colleen"—here McTee set his teeth, but Harrigan went on—"I hate McTee, and it's for your sake that I hate him. And it's for your sake that I'm goin' to forget it for a while. There's throuble abroad—there's a cloud over this ship an' a curse on it—"

"What he means to say," broke in McTee, and then he became aware that she had not heard him speak, and he saw her smiling as she drank in the musical brogue of the Irishman.

"A curse on it, acushla, an' a promise av death that only two shtrong men can save you from—an' McTee is shtrong—so I've put away desire av killin' him till we get you safe an' sound to the shore, colleen, acushla; but ye must trust in us, an' follow us as ye love your life an' as I love ye!"

She straightened in her chair and turned her eyes toward McTee.

"And you cannot tell me what the danger is?"

"We cannot," he answered, "but you must pay no attention to anything that happens or to anything that is said to you by others. There are only two men on the *Heron* whom you can trust—and here we are. But there may be wild happenings on the *Heron*. Keep your courage and trust hi Angus McTee and—"

"And Harrigan," broke in the Irishman quickly, with a glare at the captain.

She reached an impulsive hand to both of them, and they met the clasp, keeping, as it were, one eye upon her and one eye of hate upon each other.

She said, and her voice was low and musical with exultation: "I've no care what happens. I know we shall pull through safely. The three of us—Dan, Angus—we lived through the storm when the *Mary Rogers* sank, we lived on the island and survived, we reached the *Heron* in safety, and as long as we stay together, we'd be safe if the whole world were against us. Don't you feel it?"

She rose, and they stood up, towering above her, while she went on in a voice trembling somewhat: "But we must not be seen together if all these dangers threaten us; they must not know that the three of us are like one great heart."

They stepped back, and McTee pulled open the door, but still she retained their hands, and now she raised them both to her lips with a gesture so swift that they could not resist it.

"Both of you," she said; "God bless you both!"

CHAPTER 31

SHE RELEASED their hands; the door closed upon them; they stood facing each other on the deck in the dark.

"McTee," said Harrigan with deep emotion, "we're swine. We were about to fight before—her."

"Harrigan," said McTee, "we *are* swine. But when the time comes, we'll make up for it to her. If you hear a word in the forecastle, let me know about it; if I hear a word in the captain's cabin, I'll send for you. I may be wrong. Henshaw may be in his right senses. We'll see. In the meantime there are just the two of us, Harrigan, and against us there's a mutinous crew on one side and a mad captain, I think, on the other."

"There's no use in thinkin'," said Harrigan; "when the time comes, we'll fight. So long, Angus. When the trouble starts, our assemblin' point is Kate."

And he went forward to the forecastle. In the morning he discovered what he wanted to know. The men were aloof from him. He was conscious of eyes upon him whenever his back was turned, but while he faced them, no one would meet his glance.

In some way Hovey had learned that Harrigan was no longer to be trusted as a member of the mutineers, and he must have spread his tidings among the rest of the sailors. What he sensed in those covert glances, however, was not an immediate danger, but rather a waiting—an expectancy, and he deduced rightly that they would not attempt to lay a hand upon him until the mutiny was started. Then he would be reserved for some lingering death as a traitor doubly dyed.

While they were eating breakfast, Hovey came in late with the word that during the night someone had tampered with the dynamo, and the result was that the ship must complete her voyage without electric lights and—far more important—without the use of the wireless. Sam Hall started to blurt a comment on this, but a glance from Hovey silenced him. It was plain that the bos'n would risk no conversation from his blunt sailors while Harrigan was in earshot. The Irishman hurried through his breakfast and took his bucket and scrubbing brush toward the bridge, for he had many questions to ask McTee. He had scarcely left the forecastle when Hovey said to Garry Cochrane: "Watch the door. I've got something important to say."

Cochrane took up the designated position, and Hovey went on: "Lads, I've bad news, bad and good news together. The boats are gone—though who the devil destroyed them we don't know—and now the wireless is destroyed. The boats are a big loss, for now we'll have to rig up some sort of a raft to make shore when we beach the *Heron* . The busting of the wireless almost balances that loss. Now we're sure they can't slip out any quick wireless call that would bring a dozen ships after us. Bad news and good news together; and here's some more of the same kind.

"Henshaw has made up his mind to give Kamasura the whip. You know what that means? Well, I'll tell you. It means that after the first dozen strokes—as Borgson will lay them on—Kamasura will break down and tell everything we don't want him to say. Understand? With the cabin warned of what we're going to do, what chance would we have to take them? So we'll hang around close, lads, and the minute Kamasura opens his face to say the wrong thing, we'll rush 'em— are you with me? And go for two men first—Black McTee and Harrigan. With them out of the way we'll simply chew up the rest. Try to take the others alive, but don't waste any time with McTee and the Irishman. You can lay to it before you start that they'll never be taken till they're dead."

For some minutes he talked on, appointing to each man or group of men the work he would be expected to perform when Hovey gave the signal to attack, which would be one long blast on his whistle.

While they planned, Harrigan had reached the bridge and found McTee impatiently awaiting him.

"You're late," frowned the Scotchman. "What's happened in the forecastle?"

"Black looks on all sides, and no talk," said Harrigan.

"A falling barometer," nodded McTee, "and things are just as bad in the cabin. You've heard about the wireless breaking?"

"I have. What does it mean?"

"It may have been done by the mutineers. I doubt it. But that isn't all that's happened. This is a pretty cool day for the tropics."

Harrigan stared at him, baffled by the sudden change of the conversation.

"It is cool," he assented.

"But in the fireroom it's hotter than it's been at any time since the *Heron* started on this trip. The second assistant came up to complain to Henshaw, and I heard them.

"'There's something wrong with the air shafts,' he said to White Henshaw.

"'Look here,' said Henshaw, 'I've had enough grumbling from the fireroom. Put a fan in the air shaft, and don't come up here again with any nonsense. D'you expect to find cool breezes in the South Seas? No, they're hot as fire—hot as fire—hot as fire!'

"He repeated those words three times over in a way that made my flesh creep, and then he laughed. Even the second saw that something was wrong. He took a long look at Henshaw, and then he went out with his head down."

"What did it all mean?" asked Harrigan.

"I don't know. I don't dare think what it means. But if my guess is right, then the *Heron* is a lot nearer hell than even you and I expected. Look, there goes Fritz Klopp, the first assistant engineer. I'll wager he's got another complaint about the heat in the fireroom."

They watched Klopp go into the captain's cabin, waited a moment, and then the door flew open and Klopp sprang out and fled aft like a man pursued. Henshaw came to the open door and peered after the engineer and laughed silently.

McTee muttered: "That's the way the devil laughs when he watches the damned souls pass by."

Here Henshaw glanced up and saw them watching him from the bridge. His face altered suddenly to a malevolence so terrible that both the men stepped back. Harrigan was trembling like a hysterical girl. He looked in the face of McTee and saw that the Scotchman had blanched. For a long moment they exchanged glances, and then McTee went down from the bridge and entered the cabin.

Henshaw was not there. He had evidently gone into the inner room, and McTee sat down to wait. The time had come for him to ask questions, and he was nerving himself for the ordeal. His plans were disturbed by a muffled sound from the inner cabin, a sound so unusual that McTee stiffened in his chair with horror and then rose slowly.

Tiptoe he stole across the floor and laid a hand lightly on the knob of the door of the captain's private room. It turned easily without any creak, and the door opened a few inches. There sat Henshaw with his back to McTee, leaning over a table. Gold pieces were spilled loosely across the surface of the wood—possibly the contents of three or four of those small canvas bags—and Henshaw leaned forward with his forehead resting upon the glittering yellow coins and one hand clutching a quantity of them. His other hand held a photograph of the dead Beatrice. The sound continued. It was the low sobbing of the captain, a hoarse and horrible murmur.

McTee closed the door and went back onto the deck, for he suddenly understood the futility of questions. Harrigan, in the meantime, had waited for the return of McTee, and when the latter did not come, the Irishman lingered on the bridge for an hour or more, pottering about with his brush in a pretense of finishing up a perfect job. His attention was drawn then by a gathering crowd and bustle in the waist of the ship between the wheelhouse and the forecastle. The entire crew of the *Heron* seemed to be mustering, with the exception of those needed to keep the engines running. They stood in a circle, leaving the cover of the hatch clear.

He hurried down to witness the ceremony, and as he reached the waist, he saw Henshaw take up his position with folded arms in the very center of the hatch. A moment later Kamasura was led up by Eric Borgson and Jan Van Roos.

The two mates, under the direction of Henshaw, lashed the Japanese face down upon the hatch, pulling his arms and legs taut with ropes that fastened to the bolts on all sides of the hatch cover.

When he was securely tied, Kamasura was stripped to the waist, and then Harrigan saw Borgson, grinning evilly, step up with a long whip in his hand. It was a blacksnake, heavily loaded and stiff at the butt and tapering gradually to a slender, supple, snakelike body, with a thin, sinister lash. Borgson whirled the whip around his head to get its balance. Henshaw stepped back, still with folded arms.

"This fellow Kamasura," he announced to the crew, "has blown up the boats of the *Heron* . There's no doubt of it. Borgson caught him almost in the act. I could do worse things than this to Kamasura, but I've decided to flog him until he confesses."

There was not a word of answer from the crew; they waited, hushed, ominous. A whisper sounded in the ear of Harrigan, who stood with gritting teeth and clenched hands.

It was McTee who murmured: "Hold onto yourself, Harrigan. Our time hasn't come."

"I'll hold onto myself all right," said Harrigan, "but look at the crew."

In fact, there was something more deadly than any snarling of a crowd in this unnatural silence of many men. Also they were not looking at Kamasura; they were staring, every man, at the bos'n, who stood with his whistle hanging from a cord around his neck.

"Begin!" said Henshaw.

The blacksnake whistled around the head of the third mate and there was a long scream from Kamasura—but the blacksnake only cracked loudly in the air. Borgson laughed with a hideous delight. Harrigan, sickly white, bowed his head. Again the blacksnake whirled and again it cracked, but this time on naked flesh, and the scream of Kamasura was like the cut of a knife.

Again, again, and again the blacksnake fell, and now Kamasura twisted his head toward the captain and cried in a voice made thin by pain and rage at once: "I confess! Captain, let me speak!"

At a gesture from Henshaw, the third mate reluctantly stepped back, drawing the lash of the blacksnake slowly through his hands with a caressing touch. Van Roos, the color completely gone from his usually blooming cheeks, cut the ropes, and Kamasura rose, facing the captain. He extended a naked, trembling arm toward Hovey.

"Mutiny!" he yelled. "The whole crew—the whole forecastle—mutiny, Cap'n Henshaw! I know—"

The piercing whistle of the bos'n cut into his speech, and the crew rolled forward over the hatch with a single shout that might have come from one throat except for its shrill volume.

CHAPTER 32

"IT'S COME!" cried Harrigan to McTee. "Kate!"

But even as he whirled, two sailors leaped on him from behind and bore him to the deck. At the same time a gun flashed in the hand of Henshaw, and he fired twice into the onrushing host. Two men crumpled up on deck and the others gave back a little—they were glad to turn to the easier prey of Van Roos and Borgson, who were instantly overpowered, while Henshaw, with brandished revolver, made his way toward the main cabin.

The second and smaller rush of the mutineers had been toward Harrigan and McTee, where the two men stood together. Harrigan, taken from behind, went down at once and then grappled with his assailants before they could use their knives. McTee stood over the struggling three and smote right and left among the mutineers. A knife caught his shirt at the shoulder and ripped it to the waist; a club whizzed past his head, but his great fists smashed home on face and head and sent men staggering and sprawling back. The confusion gave him an instant of freedom in a small circle, and he leaned and caught one of Harrigan's assailants by the heels. It was a little man, a withered fellow scarcely five feet tall and literally dried up by the tropic heat. He was wrenched from his hold, heaved into the air, and then whirled about the head of McTee like a mighty bludgeon. As the sailors rushed again, that living club smashed against them and flung them back. Even to the herculean strength of McTee it was a prodigious feat, but the danger gave him for the moment the power of a madman. Twice he swung the shrieking little sailor, and twice that body smashed back the attack, while Harrigan leaped to his feet in time to knock down a man who sprang at McTee from behind with a brandished knife.

All this had occurred in the space of half a dozen seconds; the first rush of the mutineers was spent; before they could lunge forward again, McTee flung the half-lifeless body of his human weapon into the midst of the crowd and, turning with Harrigan at his shoulder, they sprang up the ladder to the main cabin door.

Hovey was screaming commands over the din; the crowd rushed after the fugitives.

Harrigan shouted at McTee: "Get Kate! Take her aft to the wireless house! I'll hold 'em here a minute and then join you!"

McTee nodded and tore down the deck toward Kate's cabin, while Harrigan pulled the knife of Kamasura from his trousers and thrust it in the face of the first man up the ladder. The blade slashed him from nose to cheekbone, and he toppled back with a yell, bearing with him in the fall the two men immediately below. Harrigan glanced across to the other ladder on the farther side of the deck, and saw Kate and McTee running aft. He turned and raced after them.

The wireless house was their one hope. There the sea would be at their backs, and the only approach for the mutineers in their rush would be up the ladders reaching from the deck below; the main cabin, on the other hand, had half a dozen places from which it could be assailed. This had been instantly seen by the other officers, and when Harrigan reached the ladder to the deck at the other end of the cabin, he saw Salvain standing in front of the wireless house, Kate and McTee in the act of climbing the steps from the waist, and White Henshaw, with his hair blowing, following hard in their tracks.

Harrigan reached the waist at a leap, and in another moment joined the survivors in the shelter of the wireless house—Kate, McTee, Henshaw, Salvain, and Sloan, a party of six. They were safe for the moment, for the mutineers would certainly never venture an attack against the wheelhouse, where they could be beaten from the ladders by the defendants, but they were safe without food, without water.

Then, as they stared hopelessly across the waist, they saw three men led across the rear promenade of the main cabin. Their hands were tied behind them, and they were kicked forward by the mutineers, first Jacob Van Roos—they could note his pallor even at that distance—then Eric Borgson, scowling and defiant, and dragged along by the men of the forecastle; and last came Douglas Campbell, surrounded by the firemen. Finally, Jerry Hovey shouted across the waist:

"Black McTee! Oh, Black McTee!"

The Scotchman raised his hand as a token that he heard.

"You're done for, McTee, you and all the rest. You're bound to starve, and when you're weak, we'll come and carry you forward, and you'll die by inches as the other three are going to die; but if you want to live—you and the girl and all of you, give us White Henshaw to treat as he ought to be treated. Give us him, an' the rest of you'll be saved. If you won't trust us, we'll bring you food and water enough to keep you alive till we reach shore. Give us Henshaw and—"

He broke off, for he heard the harsh, ringing laughter of White Henshaw. The captain held up his revolver.

"No use, Hovey," he called. "I fired five shots, but I saved one for myself. Ha, ha, ha!" And his mirthless cackle broke out once more.

"Look!" cried Kate, and pointed at the captain.

Down the left side of Henshaw, bright against the white of his coat, was a rapidly growing stain of red. They could see the small slit in the cloth where a knife thrust had entered his side, but the old buccaneer would give no sign of his injury. He waved his gun toward Kate as she advanced an impulsive step toward him.

"Keep back!" he commanded. "Woman and man, I trust none of you. Give me distance or I'll use this bullet on the first of you and give what's left of me to the sea."

"By the Lord, he's wounded!" cried Harrigan. "Steady, old heart of oak, you've nothing to fear from us. Hovey! Oh-h, Hovey, we'll see you damned before we give up the captain!"

The bos'n, choking with his fury, shook his clenched fist at them and disappeared into the cabin.

"Now lie down," said McTee to the captain, "and we'll fix you up. Are you badly hurt?"

"Enough to finish me," said Henshaw calmly, "but keep off! I'll have none of you! None of your tricks!"

His old body was trembling with the pain of his wound, but the hand which held the gun leveled on McTee was as steady as a rock. Kate pushed McTee aside and turned a glance of scorn on the others.

"You'd let him die among you—for fear of an old man and his wretched revolver?"

She faced Henshaw.

"Go into the wireless house, Captain Henshaw, and I will go in alone with you. If you don't trust me, you can keep your revolver at my breast while I dress your wound—but see!—you will bleed to death in a short time!"

He laughed again, saying: "Girl, there's nothing between heaven and hell that can make me die by anything but fire—fire at sea—blue fire."

She whitened at sight of his frenzied, yellow face, and then she saw Harrigan slipping around to take the captain from the rear. He saw the shadow of the Irishman just too late, and whirled with a curse at the same time that Harrigan's iron hand seized the gun. For an instant he struggled, but those mighty arms gathered him as easily as a woman lifts a stubborn child, and he was carried into the wireless house and placed on Sloan's bunk. As soon as he discovered that he was helpless in their hands, he ceased struggling and lay without a motion while they tore away his coat and shirt and Kate started to dress the deep, ugly wound.

She had scarcely finished when a shout, or rather a scream, from fifty throats brought them running out of the wireless house. Again and again that cry was repeated from the main cabin, and they could not tell whether it was despair or agony that inspired it.

Neither of these emotions caused it. All that time Hovey had been kneeling in front of the captain's safe working at the combination, for he had seen Henshaw open it several times and thought that he could imitate the captain's motions. But he failed. Around him packed the sailors in both cabins, a serried mass of intent faces and burning eyes. But at last Hovey stood up and announced his failure—he could not work the combination. Then came that yell which those in the wireless house heard, a cry of mingled rage and disappointment. Gold in untold quantities was here just within their reach—and yet just beyond it. A few inches of steel kept the gold safe.

Men beat it with their bare hands in a senseless fury, till Garry Cochrane slipped through the dense mass of sailors.

"I know something about locks. What do I get, lads, if I open this one?"

"Five shares!"

"Ten shares!"

"Ten shares!" nodded Cochrane. "Good! Now keep still. I need quiet."

They were mute; not a breath was drawn; they scarcely dared move their eyes lest he should be disturbed. Cochrane touched the lock lightly and then rubbed his fingertips vigorously back and forth on the carpet— anything to stimulate those fine nerves which are as valuable to some criminals as eyes are to normal people.

With ear pressed close to the combination, he turned it slowly, by delicate degrees, waiting for the telltale click. They saw him set his teeth and grow eager as a hound on a scent of blood; they saw the fingers move rapidly and nervously, and then came a click which was audible through the entire room, and the door of the safe swung open. Still no one stirred, no one breathed. He took out a small canvas bag, he untied the top, he spilled the contents out, and then they saw bright gold, gold which inspires, and gold which destroys, gold the tempter and the murderer.

A wild scramble followed. They swept the gold up in handfuls and tossed it into the air, laughing like madmen as the light gleamed on the yellow surfaces. And at length when they were wearied of touching it and caressing it, Hovey apportioned the spoils: to Cochrane, by common assent, the ten shares, a fortune; to Sam Hall, Kyle, and Flint, two shares each, for they had been leaders in the fight; to himself ten shares, also by universal voice, and to each of the others, forty in all, his portion.

There was no fighting or complaint over the division of the spoils. What difference did a few hundred pieces here or there matter? Gold in floods, gold in oceans, was before them, and each man gathered his own share close.

But where there is gold there is death. One of the firemen said in the ear of Hovey: "The second assistant—Fritz Klopp—he is dying."

It was upon Klopp that they depended for the running of the Heron. Hovey merely laughed: "Carry him in here. He'll come to life when he sees this!"

They had left Klopp lying on the deck. He had been one of the first to leap at White Henshaw, and a bullet from the captain's revolver had torn its way through his lungs; his eyes were glazing fast when two of the firemen carried him into the outer cabin of White Henshaw and placed him in an armchair beside the desk.

"How are you, Klopp?" asked Hovey.

"I am dying," answered the engineer, and a faint pink froth bubbled to his lips as he spoke.

Hovey merely laughed; he spilled Klopp's share of the gold across the surface of the table, a gleaming pile.

"How are you, Klopp?" he repeated.

"I will live," croaked the dying man, and instantly his clutches were among the hundreds of coins, and his red mouth grinned with a ghastly joy. He had forgotten death.

"You will live!" rumbled Sam Hall. "A man would be a fool to die when there's so much money in sight. Where's your hurt?"

"I have no hurt," whispered Klopp hoarsely, "but I'm on fire inside. Water! Something to drink!"

"Something to drink, but not water," responded Hovey. "Hey, Kamasura! Drink! Whisky!"

Instantly Kamasura, who had evidently anticipated the order, came staggering into the room with a literal armful of bottles. Hovey himself brought a glass and placed it in the hand of Klopp and filled it to the brim.

"Drink!" shouted Hovey, and sprang upon a chair so that all might see him. "Drink to Fritz Klopp! White Henshaw potted him, but he laughs at death, and he'll bring the old *Heron* to shore. Here's to Fritz Klopp!"

Many a glass was raised high. They drank with a shout of applause to Fritz Klopp, who sat without stirring his glass, one hand upon it, and the other buried among the heaps of gold, his head resting against the back of the chair, and his red mouth still ajar in that horrible grin.

"What ye laughin' at?" yelled Sam Hall in his ear. "Are ye drunk at the sight of the money, man?"

There was no answer. Hall caught him by the shoulder to rouse him, but Klopp's head merely sagged far to one side, though his glazed eyes still seemed to be fixed upward upon the same spot on the ceiling at which he had been staring before.

"What is it?" cried one or two. "What does he see?"

"Death, you fools!" answered Hovey. "And how the devil will we bring the *Heron* to land without an engineer?"

CHAPTER 33

"MAKE CAMPBELL run the ship," said Cochrane.

"You can't *make* a Scotchman do anything."

"Persuade him, then," went on Cochrane. "He'd sell his soul for a drink of that whisky. But if you can't persuade him, I'd trust to those fellows to make him do what you want."

And he pointed to the firemen.

"I'll let 'em play their little game till they're tired of it," answered Hovey, "an' then we'll bring up Campbell an' try what we can do with him."

The "little game" had now become a wild debauch. Except for the few unfortunates who had been detailed by Hovey to guard the prisoners and see that the fugitives in the wireless house made no attempt to rush the main cabin as a forlorn hope, every man of the crew was gathered in the captain's cabins or on the deck nearby. The fireroom was deserted; the engines stopped; the *Heron* floated idly on the swell of the sea; but heedless of this the mutineers celebrated their victory.

They divided their attention between drinking and gambling. They seemed feverishly eager to throw away their piles of gold. Some of them flipped coins at ten dollars a throw. Others tossed dice. One group of four sat around a greasy pack of cards betting on which man would draw the first jack.

Those who lost did not envy the winners. They looked about; gold was on all sides, heaps of it; if their hands were empty, their eyes were rich. Sam Hall lost his entire share within an hour, betting recklessly. He approached a gigantic fireman who squatted by the wall with a canvas bag clutched in one hand and a broken bottle in the other. The whisky had run out on the floor, but the fellow was too far gone to know the difference, and from time to time he raised the empty bottle to his lips.

"Money gone," said Hall. "Gimme!" And he held out his hand.

The fireman, with a vast grin, delved his hand into the bag and brought it forth loaded with gold, which Hall took without a word and returned to his game of rolling dice, one throw at five hundred dollars a throw. In ten minutes he went back to the fireman with a double handful of corns.

"Principal an' interest," grunted the big sailor, and dumped his gold into the canvas bag which, filled to overflowing, spilled a dozen coins upon the floor.

The fireman, with a groan of dull content, slipped prone on the floor and was instantly asleep, embracing the canvas bag in both arms. Every man in the crew was in a somewhat similar condition, saving Hovey, with his gray-blue, steady eyes, and Cochrane, with his glittering, shifty black. These two watched the rest descend toward swinish unconsciousness; they saw, and waited coolly, and now and then glanced at each other with faint smiles of understanding.

Somewhere in the waist of the ship Jacob Flint was singing shrill songs of infinite profanity, but otherwise there was no sound on the *Heron* as the sun went down, and all night long the old freighter wallowed sluggishly up and down on the waves, as if she waited for dawn before resuming her journey toward the shore.

There was a wisdom, however, in Hovey's laxness of discipline during the first day of his mastery. The next morning the men slept late, sprawling about the deck, and Hovey and Cochrane first roused ominous Jacob Flint and Sam Hall and Kyle. With this nucleus of five mighty men, men to be feared on land or sea, Hovey started to rouse the rest of the mutineers. They woke cursing and sad of stomach and head, and to the first orders they responded with cursing; the reply was a sledge-hammer blow from the fist of Hall or Kyle, and while the man lay on the deck, it was explained curtly and forcibly to him that while the *Heron* was at sea, he would have to obey Bos'n Hovey; but as soon as the ship reached land, each man could be his own master.

First of all the firemen were commanded to the hole to get up steam, but when this was done, it was found that there was some minor trouble with the machinery. An engineer was needed; Hovey, with Cochrane, Flint and Hall beside him, sent for Campbell, and retired to the cabin to await his coming.

There sat the body of Fritz Klopp as it had remained ever since the beginning of the revels the day before, grinning up at the ceiling. Hall and Flint raised the body, and the clutching fingers were found to be frozen by death immovably around a whole handful of gold. As Hall suggested, this would serve as lead to take him to the bottom of the sea. The others applauded the thought, and with his hand still full of gold, they carried Fritz Klopp to the rail and dumped him into the water.

As they re-entered the cabin, Campbell was kicked in from the opposite door. His hands were manacled behind him, and the force of the kick, together with a sway of the ship, threw him off his balance. He crashed on his face at the feet of Hovey. The bos'n grew positively pale with pleasure. He selected a cigar from an open box on the table and lighted it leisurely.

At last he ordered: "Pick him up."

The chief engineer was jerked to his feet and stood with a trickle of blood running down from his split lip. His face was rather purple than red, and the dark pouches underneath his eyes told the horror of the night he had passed. Nevertheless, the eyes themselves were bright.

Far away, half heard, and drowned by any noise near at hand, was a sound of singing. It was Black McTee in the wireless house, half maddened by thirst and hunger and despair, and singing in defiance songs of bonny Scotland.

"There's been trouble aboard, chief," he said, "but now trouble's over. All over! We want you to take charge of the engines again and bring us to shore."

Campbell waited, not as if he had not heard. In spite of himself, Hovey stirred a trifle and grew uneasy. From a corner of the room he picked up a canvas bag and dropped it with a melodious jingling on the table in front of the engineer.

"This is your share," he said.

Campbell smiled faintly.

"And this," said Hovey, with a glance at his companions.

The smile had not altered on the lips of the Scotchman.

"With this money," said Hovey, forcing himself to remain calm, "you can retire from active work. You can get yourself a little place on the coast somewhere"—he had heard Campbell name some of his dreams—"and have a little cellar full of the right stuff, and have your friends run out to see you now an' then, an' talk over things that're goin' on at sea—where you ain't."

Here he placed a third bag of money on the table.

"You could do all that and more, chief—a lot more—with this money."

Hovey cut the lace which tied the mouth of one of the bags; he poured the gleaming contents across the table.

"Well?" he asked softly.

"Damn you!" whispered Campbell, and then, "You fool, am I not Scotch?"

"At least," went on the bos'n easily, "think it over, chief, and while you're thinkin', what d'you say to a drop of the real stuff?"

Campbell had not tasted either food or liquid since early the day before, and his eyes were moist as they stared at the two bottles.

"Set his hands free," said Hovey, "so that the chief can drink. We ain't half-bad fellers, Campbell; but we've got good cause for raisin' the hell you've seen on the *Heron.*"

While he spoke, the arms of Campbell were set free, and glasses were shoved toward him, one full of Scotch and the other of seltzer. The mutineers were already raising their drinks for a toast when Campbell took his with a violently trembling hand. But as he lifted the liquor, he was fully conscious for the first time of a singing which had been faint in the air for some time, the songs of Black McTee in the wireless house, and now the big-throated Scotchman swung into a new air, plaintive and rapid in cadence, a death song and a war song at once, the speech of Bruce before Bannockburn, as Burns conceived it. Loud and true rang the voice of Black McTee, breaker of men:

"Scots wha hae wi' Wallace bled, Scots wham Bruce hae aften led, Welcome to your gory bed, Or to victory!"

And the hand of Campbell checked on its way to his lips. "We're lookin' in your eyes, chief," said Hovey. And the song broke in:

"Wha would be a traitor slave, Let him turn and flee!"

Campbell was staring at the wall like one who sees a vision but cannot make out its meaning.

The voice of Black McTee swelled high and strong:

"Wha for Scotland's king and law Freedom's sword will strongly draw, Free-men stand and freemen fa', Let him on wi' me!"

And the glass dropped from the lips of the Scotchman. It crashed against the hard floor. Broad Scotch was on his tongue.

"I canna drink wi' murderers!" he cried.

"Damn you!" said Hovey, and drove his fist into Campbell's face, hurling him to the deck.

The manacles were clapped on his wrists again; he was dragged once more to his feet.

"Take him out," said Hovey to the grinning sailors who had lingered in the door. "Take him back to the waist of the ship before the wireless house. Wait for me there. And see that Van Roos and Borgson are brought there also."

CHAPTER 34

AS CAMPBELL was dragged away, the bos'n said to his companions: "Now, lads, you see where Campbell stands!"

They growled for answer.

"But I'll get him!" went on Hovey. "I'm going to kill Van Roos and Borgson by inches before his eyes. And when he sees 'em die—they'll have to die, anyway, before we reach shore—Campbell will be water in our hands. He'll see 'em die, an' them in the wireless house will see 'em die. Their throats are thick with thirst by now. We'll show 'em water an' food, an' offer it to 'em if they'll give up Henshaw. If they won't, we'll show 'em how we'll kill 'em when they're too weak to resist. They'll see a sample in Van Roos and Borgson. Every yell they let out'll be an argument for us. We'll have Henshaw before the day's done."

Sam Hall pushed his thick fingers slowly through his hair, stupefied by this careful cruelty, and even the one eye of Jacob Flint grew dim, but Garry Cochrane slapped the bos'n on the shoulder heartily.

"Jerry," he said, "you got the makin's of a great man. Let's go start the fun."

On the way aft they passed the firemen sprawling on the shady side of the deck. They stumbled to their feet at sight of Hovey, and swore volubly that the hole of the ship was too hot for a man to live in it five minutes. Hovey passed them without a word. He had to tend to Campbell now, and without an engineer it was useless to work men in the fireroom.

First of all he had two buckets of water carried aft and placed just below the edge of the raised deck which supported the wireless house. There were dippers floating invitingly on the surface of the water in each bucket. Then from the galley of the ship Kamasura and Shida, the cabin boys, brought out steaming meats and cut loaves of bread and displayed the feast near the buckets of water. Upon this outlay gazed the famine-stricken fugitives, Sloan, McTee and Harrigan; Kate did not see, for she was caring for the sick captain. Hovey advanced and made a speech.

"We're actin' generous and open to you," he began. "We're offerin' you food an' water—all you want—in exchange for White Henshaw. He sold his soul to hell long ago, an' we've come to claim payment. It's overdue, that's what it is!"

"Aye, aye!" came a chorus of yells from the sailors. "White Henshaw's overdue."

"Look at this here water," went on Hovey, with a tempting wave of his hand. "Why not take this up an' help yourselves—after you've given us Henshaw?"

Sloan crowded in between Harrigan and McTee; his voice was a slavering murmur: "For pity's sake, boys, what we going to do?"

Harrigan and the big Scot exchanged glances. Faintly and slowly they smiled. There was a profound mutual understanding in that smile.

"I'm dying," went on Sloan eagerly and still in that slavering voice. "I'm burnin' up inside. For God's sake let 'em take him and finish him off!"

And always as he spoke his quick eyes went back and forth from face to face. They had neither eye nor voice for him. They turned their attention back to Hovey, who now spoke again hastily.

"But if you don't give us Henshaw, we'll take him, anyway. In one more day—or maybe two at the most—we'll come an' get you—understand? An' what we'll do to you when we get you will be this!"

He gestured over his shoulder. Eric Borgson was being led out on the deck by some of the crew.

"Look him over, Cap'n McTee. He's a big man, an' we're goin' to kill him by inches. So we're goin' to finish Van Roos—the same way. Speak out, lads; d'you want to die like these two are goin' to die, or will you turn over Henshaw—who needs killin'?"

McTee smiled benevolently down upon the upturned, furious faces of the mutineers, and muttered: "Harrigan, I could drink blood."

"An' lick your lips afther it," groaned the Irishman softly. "An' so could I, Angus! They're startin' their devil work. Let's go inside. I can't be standing the sight of it, McTee."

"Go inside an' let 'em rush the wireless house?" said McTee incredulously. "No, lad. We *got* to stay an' watch. Besides, maybe this is the way we'll all die—after we're too weak to fight 'em. And I'm rather curious to learn just how I'll die; I've always been!"

They were binding Borgson face down on the hatch.

"Look," said Harrigan. "Maybe it ain't goin' to be so bad as we thought. They're just goin' to lick Borgson the way he licked the Jap."

"They'll do more," replied McTee, shaking his head. "Henshaw and Borgson and Van Roos have really put those wild men through hell, and now they're going to get it back with interest."

In the meantime little Kamasura stepped out from the crowd. He was naked to the waist, for the raw incisions which the lash had left would not bear the weight of clothes. He carried the blacksnake in his hands, drawing it caressingly through his hands as Borgson had done. Now the tying of Borgson was completed, and the sailors spread back in a loose circle to watch their entertainment.

The Japanese took his distance carefully, shifting repeatedly a matter of inches to make sure that no stroke would be wasted. Then he whirled the blacksnake over his head. They could see Borgson wince as the lash sang above him, and the muscles of his bare back flexed and stood up in knots that glistened under the sunlight. But the stroke did not fall. Kamasura had learned the lesson of creating suspense from the very man he was now about to torture. Harrigan bowed his head in his hands.

"I can't look, McTee," he muttered. "I'm sick inside—sick—sick!"

The last words came in a growl from the hollow of his throat. The blacksnake whirled through the air again and fell with a sharp slap like two broad hands clapped together, but Borgson did not cry out. His body writhed mutely, and down his back appeared a red mark. The whip whirled again and fell, this time bringing a stifled curse for a response. Once more it whirled, and this time merely cracked in the air. Again and again an idle snap in the air. Broken by that grim suspense, Borgson yelled in terror.

Kamasura laughed and glanced at the circle of sailors like a ringmaster in a circus in search of applause. The whip now whirled rapidly over his head and fell again and again, and every stroke brought a fresh and louder scream from the mate. Another sound, rhythmic and barbarous, punctuated those shrieks of anguish. It was the singing of Kamasura, who as he wielded the lash remembered a chant of his native land and shouted it now in time with the blows of the blacksnake.

On the upper deck Sloan lay prone on his face, sobbing with terror; Harrigan kept his face hid and clutched at his head with both hands; McTee stared straight down upon the scene of the torture with burning eyes. Inside the wheelhouse Kate crouched beside the bunk on which Henshaw was stretched, staring straight above his head. The fever had deprived him of the last of his senses.

"Your hands!" he muttered at length.

She placed them upon his forehead. She had done that repeatedly during the past day, and each time the effect had been marvelously soothing to the old man. Now at the touch he drew a deep breath of relief.

"Even in hell," he whispered at length—"even in hell you come to me, Beatrice! I knew you would!"

He caught her hands at the wrists; his fingers, despite his fever, were deadly cold, and a chill ate into her blood.

"I hear them yelling—the souls of the damned," he said quietly. "You can't hear it?"

"No, no!" she said. "I cannot hear!"

"Of course not," he went on with the same lack of emotion; "for, you see, you've come from heaven, and the coolness of heaven is in your hands, Beatrice. Put them against my temples, so! For every bit of the love I have given you you are permitted to repay me with coolness— coolness and comfort in hell!"

Suddenly he broke into exultant laughter, a sound more terrible than the wild wails from the deck.

"See!" he said, and his eyes twinkled as he stretched out a gaunt arm toward a corner of the room. "There's Johnny Carson lying naked on a bed of blue fire. Ha, ha, ha! Have you been waiting long for me to come, lad?"

She shut out the hungry, hideous light of his eyes with the palms of her hands. Now the screaming on the deck ceased abruptly.

"Beatrice!" he cried with a sudden terror.

"Yes," answered Kate.

"Ah," he said, and patted her hands endearingly. "When the silence came, I feared maybe you were leaving me. You won't do that?"

"No. I'll stay."

"So! Then I'll sleep. But waken me when they begin yelling again. They thought I'd come down to the same hell I sent them to, and that they'd watch me burn. But I fooled 'em, Beatrice, by loving you. You're the chip of wood that keeps me afloat—afloat—afloat—"

And he drifted into sleep, while she leaned against the bunk, almost unconscious from fear and exhaustion.

CHAPTER 35

KAMASURA, IN nowise loath to bring his work to an end, stood back and laid on the whip with redoubled vigor. The lash spatted sharply against the raw and bleeding flesh. The screams sank into moans, and the moans in turn declined to a mere horrible gasping of the breath. Even this ceased at length, and the quivering of the body stopped. Kamasura leaned over and slipped his hand under the body in the region of the heart. When he straightened up again, he made a gesture of finality with his crimsoned hands. The mate was dead.

They cut his body loose at once and pitched him over the rail, then turned their attention to Van Roos. Sam Hall was the inspired man this time, and according to his directions they lashed the body of the big mate on the same blood-spotted hatch cover where Borgson had lain a moment before, but this time the victim was placed upon his back. Hall himself attended to the tying of Van Roos's head, and he performed his work so ably that the mate could not change his position in the least particle. He was literally swathed in ropes; so much so, in fact, that it was difficult to see how he could be tormented. Sam Hall, however, insisted that this was what he wanted, and the crew consented to let him do his work.

"You've heard something, an' you've seen something," said Hovey at this juncture to Campbell; "but what you've seen and heard isn't nothin' to what'll happen to you unless you start handling the engines of the *Heron* . Why, Campbell, I'm goin' to give you to the firemen!"

"Hovey," answered the engineer calmly, "the only place I'd run this ship would be down to hell—your home port. That's final!"

The bos'n was white with rage.

"I'd like to tear your heart out an' feed it to the fish," he said, stepping close to Campbell, and then, remembering himself, he moved back and grinned: "But the men will find something better to do with you."

He crossed the deck and held up a bucket of water toward Harrigan and McTee. He raised a dipperful and allowed it to splash back in the bucket.

"Well?" asked Hovey.

They merely stared at him as if they had not heard him speak.

"All right," said Hovey, quite unmoved, "there's plenty of time for you to make up your minds. But if you wait too long—well, we'll come and get him. And the girl, too!"

He laughed and turned away.

"I thought," muttered McTee, "that we could end it by simply dying—but I forgot the girl."

"The girl," answered Harrigan, "and—and them! She's got to die before we're too far gone. You'll do that to save her from—them?"

McTee moistened his parched lips before he could speak.

"One of us has to do it, but it can't be me, Harrigan."

"Nor me, Angus. We'll wait till tonight. Maybe a ship'll pass and see us lyin' like a derelict and put a boat aboard, eh?"

"But if no ship comes, then we'll draw straws, eh?"

"Yes."

Two sharp, sudden cries now called their attention back to the waist of the ship to the blood-stained hatch cover where Van Roos lay.

Sam Hall had approached the big mate with a knife in his hand. He kneeled beside the prostrate body and fumbled at the face an instant. No one had been able to make out the significance of his act. Then the knife gleamed, and twice he plucked with one hand and cut with the knife. The two sharp cries answered him. Then he rose; two little trickles of blood ran down the face of the mate.

"Well?" asked Jacob Flint. "When does the game begin?"

"The game is just started," said Hall, "an' the sun will do the rest. I've cut off his eyelids!"

They stared a moment in amazement, and then an understanding broke on them. Every tribe of savages in the world has been accredited with this ingenious torture which blinded their victim and usually drove him mad. The sun was now climbing the sky rapidly, and already fell on the face of the mate. The tropic sun which scorches and burns the toughest of skins was now directed full on the pupils of his eyes.

The sailors sought comfortable positions and waited for a long exhibition of pain, but they were mistaken. The torture acted far more quickly than even the whip. There was no outcry. Not once during his struggles did Van Roos make a sound from his throat, save for a quick, heavy panting. Perhaps by contrast with the yells of Borgson, which were still in the ears of the men, this silence was more horrible than the most throat-filling shrieks. They could see Van Roos twisting his head ceaselessly and vainly to escape that blinding light. His ruddy face became swollen like the features of a drowned man. And that was all that happened—only that, and the panting, the quick, choppy panting like a running man. Finally one of the sailors rose with a mallet in his hand.

"Where you goin'?" asked Hall ominously.

"Going to finish him."

Hall caught the fellow's arm.

"Listen!" he whispered, and such was the silence that the hoarse whisper was audible all over the deck. "Don't you hear?"

And with one hand he kept beat for the quick breaths of the tortured man. At that moment there was a long sigh, and the breathing stopped. Hall strode angrily forward to his victim, but when he reached the hatch, Van Roos was dead. A blood vessel must have burst in his brain, and death was as instantaneous as though a bullet had struck him. So they cut him free, and his body followed that of Borgson over the rail. Then the eyes of the mutineers turned aft toward the wireless house, and then back upon Campbell. Six victims remained. One of the firemen slipped close to Hovey on naked feet. He did not speak, but his long, thin arm pointed toward the engineer.

"Not yet," said Hovey, "not yet! Tomorrow if he doesn't give in, we'll turn you loose on him."

The fireman grinned and went back on noiseless feet to his companions to spread the good tidings. Hovey approached the wireless house.

"We've got one show left to offer, but we're savin' it till tomorrow," he said. "So brace up, hearties, and keep cheer. You'll see Campbell go a way worse than either of these tomorrow."

"Wait," called Harrigan, suddenly roused. "D'you mean to say that you'd try your hellwork on a kind man like Campbell?"

"A kind man like Campbell?" echoed Hovey, and then laughed. "A kind man?"

And he retreated with no other answer, and left the fugitives aft to the merciless, sweltering heat of the sun. By the time the sun went down, they were so fevered by the need of water that they had not the strength to bless the cool falling of the dark; they still carried the fire of the sunlight in their blood.

CHAPTER 36

"THIS MAN Campbell," said Harrigan, "he's a true man, McTee, and he stood up to White Henshaw for my sake—for the sake of me and his Bobbie Burns. They plan to take him to hell tomorrow, Angus, and I've an idea that there's one chance in the thousand that I could steal in on the dogs tonight and bring him back with me."

"Can they do anything worse to him than they're doing to us?"

"Maybe not, but my heart would lie easier, McTee. I'll wait for the fever o' the sun to go out of me head an' for the crew to get drunk an' a little drunker."

So they waited while the noise of the nightly carousal waxed high and higher, and then died away by slow degrees. At length Harrigan stood up, gripped the hand of McTee in silent farewell, heard a whispered "Good luck!" and slipped noiselessly down the ladder and started across the deck in the shadow of the rail. From any portion of the main cabin eyes might be watching him; there was only the one chance in ten that the lookout whom Hovey had certainly stationed would not perceive him as he crept along under the shadow. Accordingly he went blindly forward.

If the lookout saw him, at least there was no outcry, no general alarm. He stood flat against the wall of the main cabin at length and rehearsed a plan, listening the while to the lapping of the waves against the side of the ship. Then he stole step by step up the ladder to the upper deck. His head was already above the ladder when he heard the light padding of a bare foot and saw a figure around the corner of the cabin.

Harrigan ducked out of sight and clung to the iron rounds ready to leap up and strike if the sailor should descend the ladder, though in that case the alarm would be given and his errand spoiled; but the sailor was apparently the lookout set there by Hovey. He stayed at the head of the ladder a moment, humming to himself, and then turned and walked on his beat to the other side of the ship. Harrigan slipped onto the deck and ran noiselessly to the side of the cabin. Here he flattened himself against the wall until the sentinel had again made the turn of his beat, and as the latter moved dimly out of sight through the darkness, the Irishman stole down the deck toward the forward cabins.

The first two windows showed dark and empty; if there were anyone inside, he must be asleep in the drunken torpor into which most of the crew seemed to have fallen. The door of the third room, formerly occupied by the second mate, stood ajar, and here by the dull light of an oil lantern, he saw Campbell tied hand and foot to a chair. He was placed close to a little table whereon sat a bottle of whisky, a siphon of seltzer, a tall glass, meat, bread, water—everything, in fact, with which the senses of the starving man could be tormented. And near him, sitting with elbows spread out on the edge of the table, was one of the firemen, grinning continually as if he had just heard some monstrous joke. The expression of Campbell was just as fixed, for his small eyes shifted eagerly, swiftly, from the food to the water, and back again.

The fireman—the same tall, gaunt fellow who had demanded that Hovey turn over Campbell to him and his companions that day—now leaned forward and raised a dipper of water from a bucket which sat on the floor, and allowed it to trickle back, splashing with what seemed to Harrigan the sweetest music in the world. Hovey must have taught him that trick, and its effect upon Campbell was worse than the beating of the whips. The fireman let his head roll loosely back as he laughed, and while his head was still back and his eyes squinting shut in the ecstasy of his delight, Harrigan leaped from the shadow of the door and struck at the throat—at the great Adam's apple which shook with the laughter. The blow must have nearly broken the man's neck. His head jerked forward with a whistling gasp of breath, and as he reached for the knife on the table, Harrigan struck again, this time just behind the ear. The man slid from his chair to the floor and lay in a queer heap—as if all the bones in his body were broken.

"Harrigan! Harrigan! Harrigan!" Campbell was whispering over and over, but still his eyes held like those of a starved wolf on the food. The moment his ropes were cut, he buried his teeth in the great chunk of roasted meat.

Harrigan jerked him away and held him by main force.

"Be a man!" he whispered. "We've got to take this food and this water back to the wireless house—if we can get there with it. Take hold of yourself, Campbell!"

The engineer nodded. Voices came close down the deck; instantly Harrigan jerked up the glass globe which protected the lantern's flame and blew out the light. They crouched shoulder to shoulder.

"I thought he was in here," said a voice at the door.

"He was," answered Hovey's voice, "but I guess they took him below— they said it was too cool for him up there. Ha, ha, ha!"

Their steps disappeared down the deck. After that Harrigan dared not show a light in the cabin window. He and Campbell located the meat and bread, which were given into the engineer's keeping, while Harrigan took the bucket of water. They slipped out onto the deck and hurried aft, keeping close to the side of the cabin, for the starlight would show their figures to any watchful eyes. At the rear edge of the cabin Harrigan halted Campbell and whispered: "There's a guard here. I got past him in the dark, but two of us loaded down like this can never go unseen down that ladder. We've got to get rid of him."

And he pulled out the knife which he had kept with him ever since the outbreak of the mutiny. They waited without daring to draw breath until the sailor came padding by with his naked feet. Harrigan crept out behind him, and when the sailor turned at the rail, the Irishman leaped in and struck, not with the blade, but with the haft of the knife; he could not kill from behind.

If it had been a solid blow, the sailor would have crumpled silently as the fireman had done a few moments before, but the impact glanced and merely cut his scalp as it knocked him down. He fell with a shout which was instantly answered from the front of the ship.

"Down the ladder! Run for it!" cried Harrigan to Campbell, and as the engineer clambered down, he stood guard above.

The sailor leaped up from the deck and lunged with a knife gleaming in his hand, but Harrigan slashed him across the arm, and he fled howling into the dark. Before Hovey and his men could reach the spot, Harrigan had climbed down the ladder with his precious bucket and was fleeing aft to the wireless house.

As he reached it, lights were showing from the main cabin, and there were choruses of yells announcing the discovery that Campbell was missed. But Harrigan and the rest of the fugitives scarcely heard the sounds. The Irishman was busy measuring as carefully as he could in the dark dippers of water which the others drank.

There was no sleep that night, partly from fear lest the infuriated mutineers should at last attempt to rush the wireless house, partly because they ate sparingly but long of the meat which Harrigan carved for them, and the bread, and partly also because of a singular odor which they had not noticed when they were tortured by thirst and hunger, and which now they observed for the first time. It was peculiarly pungent and heavy with a sickening suggestion of sweetness about it. None of them could describe it, saving Harrigan, who had been much in the country and likened the odor to the smell of an old straw stack which lay molding and rotting.

It seemed to increase—that smell—during the night, probably because their strength was returning and all their senses grew more acute. It was a torrid night, without moon, so that the blanket of dark pressed the heat down upon them and seemed to stifle the very breath.

With the coming of the first light of the dawn they noticed a peculiar phenomenon. Perhaps it was because of the evaporation of water under the fire of the sun, but the *Heron* seemed to be surrounded with a white vapor which rose shimmering in the slant rays of the morning. But even when the sun had risen well up in the sky, the vapor was still visible, clinging like a wraith about the ship. They wondered idly upon it, and wondered still more at the heat, which was now intense. They were interrupted in their conjectures by the call of Kate summoning them to the wireless house where Henshaw lay apparently at the last gasp.

He had altered marvelously in the past two days. That resemblance which he had always had to a mummy was now oddly intensified, for the cheeks were fallen, the neck withered to scarcely half its former size, the eyes sunk in purple hollows. He murmured without ceasing, his voice now rising hardly above a low whisper. Kate sat beside him, passing her hands slowly over his temples, for he complained of a fire rising within his brain.

His complaints died away under her touches, and he said at last, calmly but very, very faintly: "Beatrice, there is one thing I have not yet told you."

"Yes?" she asked gently, though she averted her eyes, for all the long hours he had filled with the stories of his crimes upon earth were poured into the ear of the spirit of his Beatrice, as he thought. One last and crowning atrocity was yet to be told.

"I have left out the greatest thing of all."

He paused to smile at the memory.

"You remember Samson's death, Beatrice? And how he pulled the house down on the shoulders of his enemies?"

"Yes."

"That was a wonderful way to die—wonderful! But I, Beatrice, look at me, child!—I have surpassed Samson! Listen! You will wonder and you will admire when you hear it! When I got the word that you were dead, I knew two things: first, that the prophecy of my death at sea would come true, and secondly that my gold must perish with me. You will never guess how long I pondered over a way to destroy my gold before I died! You will think I could have simply thrown it into the sea? Yes, but the ship was filled with men ready to mutiny, and they were hungry for my wealth. They would never have allowed me to destroy that gold! So I thought of a way—ah, it was an inspiration!—by which I could destroy my body, my wealth, and the lives of all the mutineers at once. Like Samson, I would pull the house on the heads of my enemies. Ha, ha, ha!"

His laughter was rather a grimace than a sound.

He went on: "See how cunningly, how carefully I worked! First I blew up the three lifeboats so that there would be no escape for the crew. Then I tampered with the dynamo so that it burned out, and they could not send out a wireless call for help. That touch was the best of all. Well, well! Then I went down into the hold, deep down, and I started a fire in the cargo. And then—"

"Oh, my God!" stammered Sloan.

The others were white, but they gestured at Sloan to silence him. The whisper continued: "And then I knew that they were done for. The wheat would not break into a sudden flame, but it would smolder and glow and spread from hour to hour and from day to day. The crew would know nothing of it for a long time. But when they guessed at what was happening, they would open the hatches to fight the fire with water. Then what would happen? Ah, my dear, there was the crowning touch; for when they opened the hatches, the current of air would feed the fire and the ship would be instantly in flames. And so they would burn like dogs with water, water all around them, and no boats to put off in—no boats. Ha, ha, ha!"

He choked with his laughter and gasped for breath.

"If it were possible for a bodiless spirit to perish, I should think that I am dying twice, Beatrice. The air is thick—this air of hell!"

He broke off short in his whispering and raised himself suddenly to an elbow. With the coming of death his voice grew strong and rang clearly: "They are in the corners—they are coming closer! Beatrice! Brush them away with your fingers as cold as snow. Beatrice, oh, my dear!"

And he was dead as he fell back on the bunk.

Sloan was already on the deck outside the wireless house, shrieking with all the power of his lungs: "Fire! Fire! The wheat in the hold!"

CHAPTER 37

AND AS Harrigan and McTee, followed by Kate and Campbell, ran out to the open air, they saw the crowd of the mutineers surge across the waist toward Sloan with upturned faces, wondering, and ready for terror. Hovey broke through their midst.

"Hovey!" shouted McTee. "Look at the mist over the sides! Draw a breath; smell of it! It is fire! Henshaw has set fire in the hold!"

It was plain to every brain in the instant. To every man came the thought of the complaints of the firemen concerning the heat in the hold of the *Heron*; the noxious odor like musty straw; the warmth, the deadly warmth of the decks. A volcano smoldered beneath them, and the mist was the sign of the coming outbreak of flames. And the mutineers stood mute, gaping at one another, looking for some hope, some comfort, and finding the same question repeated in every eye. McTee climbed down the ladder to the waist, followed by the rest of the fugitives. Ten minutes before they would have been torn to pieces by the wolf pack. Now no man had a thought for anything save his own death.

"Hovey," ordered McTee in his voice of thunder, "tell these fellows they must obey my voice from now on."

They roared, snatching at this ghost of a hope: "We will! We'll follow Black McTee! Hovey has brought us to hell!"

In a moment everyone was in frantic motion. Campbell started for the engine room to see what had caused the stopping of the ship. McTee himself, followed by Harrigan and the stokers, went down to the fireroom. It was fiery hot there, indeed. When the Scotchman swung down the ladder into the hole, it was like a blast from a furnace, and the air was foul with the nauseating odor of the smoldering wheat. The men gasped and struggled for breath, and yet they began to work without complaint.

All hands set to. The fires were shaken down and started afresh; the coal shoveled out from the bunkers. Then a fireman collapsed without a cry of warning. They carried him out to the upper air, and brought down two of the sailors to take his place. And the sailors went without a murmur. They were fighting for the one chance in ten thousand, the chance of bringing the ship to shore before the fire burst out in flame which would lick the *Heron* from one end to the other within an hour.

McTee went up to the bridge to take the bearings and lay the course. By the time his reckonings were completed, steam was up; Campbell had remedied the trouble in the engine room; the propeller began to turn, and a yell went up from the ship and tingled to heaven. When McTee came down from the bridge to the waist, leaving Hovey at the wheel, a dozen of the tars gathered about the new skipper, weeping and shouting, for in their eyes he was the deliverer, it was he who was giving them the fighting chance to live.

And how they fought! There was something awe-inspiring and almost be-yond the human in the fury with which they labored. It was in the fireroom that their chief difficulty lay. The fireroom of a large steamer is a veritable furnace, and when to this heat was added that from the hold of the ship, it was truly a miracle that any living thing could exist there.

But Harrigan was in charge. When men wilted and pitched to their faces on the sooty, dusty floor, he trussed them under one arm and bore them up to the air. Then he went back and drove them on again. Before the end of that day, however, with the coast still a full thirty-hour run ahead of them, it became liter-ally impossible to continue longer in the fireroom. But Harrigan would not leave. He had a hose introduced into the hold. The men worked absolutely naked with a stream of water playing on them. Now and again when one of them collapsed, Harrigan snatched the fire bar or the shovel from the hands of the worker and labored furiously until another substitute was found.

The necessity of his presence was amply demonstrated that night. The Irish-man was too exhausted to continue another minute, and the men helped him to the deck and sluiced buckets of salt water over his great, trembling body. To keep the men at work, Campbell went down in the hole.

They had to carry him up in half an hour. Then McTee tried his hand. He stood the heat as well as Harrigan, but he could not inspire such daredevil en-thusiasm in the men. They missed the raucous, cheery voice of Harrigan; they missed the inspiring sight of that flame-red hair; and they missed above all his peculiar driving force. In other words, when Harrigan came among them, they felt *hope* , and when a man has hope, he will work on in the face of death.

And at last McTee came up and begged Harrigan to go back. He went, and found an empty fireroom and dying fires. He ran back to the deck, and at his shout the dead veritably rose to life. Men staggered to their feet to follow him below. Every man on the ship took his turn. Hovey came down and passed coal; McTee came down and wielded the fire bar, doing the labor of three men while he could endure.

And the *Heron* drove on toward the shore. The morning passed; the after-noon wore away. It was a matter of hours now before the shore would be in sight, and McTee spread this news among the crew. He sent little Kamasura and Shida, the cabin boys, running here and there saying to every man they passed: "Four hours! Four hours! Four hours!" And then: "Three hours! Three hours! Three hours!"

And the crew swallowed whisky neat and returned to the fireroom.

At sunset, dim as a shadow, a thing to be guessed at rather than known, the man on the bridge sighted land. The word spread like lightning. The staggering workers in the fireroom heard and joined the cheer which Harrigan started. Then the catastrophe came.

A torch of red fire licked up the stern of the ship; the flames had eaten their way out to the open air!

It was the quick action of McTee which kept the panic from spreading to the hold of the ship at once and bringing up every one of the workers from the fireroom. He gathered the sailors on deck who had strength enough left to walk, and they made a line and attacked the flames with buckets of water. There was, of course, no possibility of quelling the fire at its source, for by this time the hold of the ship where the wheat was stowed must have been one glowing mass of smoldering matter. Yet they were able, for a time, to keep the course of the fire from spreading over the decks of the ship.

With this work fairly started, McTee ran back to the forward cabin and upper deck of the *Heron* and set several men to tear down some of the framework, sufficient at least to build enough rafts to maintain the crew in the water. So the three sections of the work went on—the firefighting, the lifesaving, and the driving of the ship. McTee on deck managed two ends of it; Harrigan in the fireroom handled the most desperate responsibility. It seemed as if these two men by their naked will power were lifting the lives of the crew away from the touch of death and hurling the ship toward the shore.

And now for an hour, for two hours, that ghastly labor continued. The entire stern of the *Heron* was a sheet of flames when the last workers staggered up from the fireroom, their skin seared and blistered by the terrific heat. Last of all came Harrigan, raving and cursing and imploring the men to return to their work. As he staggered up the deck, reeling and sobbing hoarsely, Kate Malone ran to him. She pointed out across the waters ahead of the ship. There rose the black shadow of the shore and under it a thin line of white—the breakers!

Now by McTee's direction the rafts were hoisted and dragged over the side of the ship, while one frail line of men remained to struggle against the encroaching flames.

They were licking into the waist of the *Heron* , and the wireless house was a mass of red; White Henshaw was burning at sea, and the prophecy was fulfilled.

The last of the rafts were hoisted overboard and half a dozen men tumbled into each. When the rest of the crew were overboard, McTee, Kate, and Harrigan, lingering behind by mutual consent, took one raft to themselves. All about them tossed the other rafts, and not one man of all the crowd had thought of the golden treasure which they were abandoning with the *Heron* . Each might be carrying a few gold pieces, but the wealth of White Henshaw would go back into the sea from which it came.

They had not abandoned the flaming ship too soon. A fresh breeze was sweeping from the ocean onto the shore, and red tongues licked about the main cabin and darted like reaching hands into the heart of the sky. By these flashes they could make out the struggling rafts where the sailors cheered and yelled in the triumph of their escape. But McTee set about erecting a jury sail.

He wrenched off two strips of board from their raft and across these he and Harrigan affixed their shirts. The same wind which had lashed the fires forward on the *Heron* now hurried the fugitives toward the shore. They had a serious purpose in outstripping the rest of the rafts, because when the mutineers reached the shore, the mood of gratitude which they held for Harrigan and McTee was sure to change, for these two men could submit enough evidence to hang them in any country in the world.

Looking back, the *Heron* was a belching volcano, which suddenly lifted in the center with the sound of a dozen siege guns in volleyed unison, and a column of fire vaulted high into the heavens. Before they reached the tossing heart of the breakers, the *Heron* was dwindling and sliding, fragment by fragment into the sea.

Through those breakers the last light from the ship helped them, and the wind tugging at their little jury sail aided to drive them on until they could swing off the raft and walk toward the beach, carrying Kate between them. On the safe, dry sands they turned, and as they looked back, the Heron slid forward into the ocean and quenched her fires with a hiss that was like a far-heard whisper of the sea.

CHAPTER 38

MEANWHILE THE shouts of the mutineers rang louder and louder as their rafts edged in toward the land, so the three turned again and made directly inland. A hundred yards from the edge of the water they were in a dense jungle such as only exists in a Central American swamp region, but they waded and splashed on, and clambered over rotten stumps, slick with wet moss, and stepped on fragments of wood that crumbled under their feet. And all the time they kept the girl between them, lifting her clear of the noisome water as much as possible.

The shouting of the mutineers, however, urged them on, and from the sound of the voices there was no doubt that Hovey and his men were combing the marsh for the fugitives. Torches had been made by the sailors, and behind them, now and then, they caught a glimpse of a winking eye of light. This drove them on, and just when the shouts of the mutineers began to die away, the marsh ended as abruptly as it had begun, and they started to climb a slope where the thicket changed to an almost open wood. The rise was not long, for after some hours of weary trudging, they reached a road.

Down this they straggled with stumbling feet. They had not spoken for nearly two hours, as though they wished to save even the breath of speech for some trial which might still await them. Kate was half unconscious with fatigue, and McTee on her left and Harrigan on her right carried most of her weight.

In this manner they came in sight of a light which developed into a low-roofed, broad house with a hospitable veranda stretching about it. They made directly for it, traversing a level field until they came to the door. McTee supported Kate while Harrigan knocked. There was silence within the house, and then a whisper, a stir, the padding of a slippered foot, and the door was jerked open. A tall man with a narrow, pointed beard appeared. He held a lantern in one hand and a pistol in the other; for those were troubled times in that republic. The light fell full on the haggard face of Kate, and the man started back.

"Enter, my children," he said in Spanish, and tossing his weapon onto a little hall table, he held out his hand to them.

With a great voice he brought his family and servants about them in a few seconds. To a wide-eyed girl with a frightened voice, he gave the care of Kate, and the two went off together. The master of the house himself attended to the needs of Harrigan and McTee.

There were few questions asked. This was a question of dire need, and the Spanish-American loves to show his hospitality. Talking was for the morning. In the meantime his guests would require what? Perhaps sleep? Perhaps a bath first? They answered him with one voice, for they both spoke a little Spanish, picked up in their wanderings. Sleep!

The next day they woke about noon to find clothes laid out for them, the immaculate white clothes which the tropics require. They were led to a high-ceilinged bathroom cool with glazed, white bricks which lined it, where the two servants poured over them bucket after bucket of cold water, and the grime of the voyage and the labors in the fireroom and the mighty weariness of their muscles disappeared little by little in slow degrees. Then a shave, then the white clothes, and they were ready for presentation to Senor Jose, Barrydos y Maria y Leon and his family.

And here was a time of many words indeed. It was McTee who told the story of the wreck, and even with his broken Spanish the tale was so vivid that Senor Jose was forced to rise and walk up and down the room, calling out upon a hundred various saints. In the end it was clear in his eyes that he had to deal with two heroes. As such they could have lived with him as honored guests forever.

Then Kate came into the room with the daughter of the house. She wore a green dress of some light material which fluttered into folds at every move. The Spaniard straightened up from his chair. The two big men followed suit, staring wide-eyed upon her. It seemed as if some miracle had been worked in her, for they looked in vain for any traces of her helpless weariness of the night before.

There was a color in her cheeks and her eyes were bright and quiet. To Senor Jose Barrydos y Maria y Leon she gave both her hands, and he bowed over them and kissed them both. His courtliness made Harrigan and McTee exchange a glance, perhaps of envy and perhaps of disquiet, for she accepted this profound courtesy with an ease as if she had been accustomed to nothing else all her life.

But what a smile there was for each of them afterward! It left them speechless, so that they glowered upon each other and were glad of the soft flow of Senor Jose's words as he led them in to the breakfast table.

And when the meal had progressed a little and some of the edge of the novelty of the situation and story had worn away, the Spaniard said: "But is it not true? Strange news floats in the air this week."

"What news?" asked Harrigan. "Our wireless was out of commission for days."

"True! Then you must learn from me?"

He drew a breath and stiffened in his chair, then with a gesture of apology and a smile he added: "Why should I hunt for pompous words? I can tell you in one phrase: the world is at war, gentlemen!"

They merely gaped upon him.

"German troops have entered Belgium; France, England, and Russia are at war with Germany and Austria!"

He waited for the astonishment to die away in their eyes.

Kate was shaking her head. "It is impossible," she said. "There may be a disturbance, but the world is past the time of great wars. Men are now too civilized, and—"

Here she stopped, for her eyes fell on the faces of Harrigan and McTee. Civilized? No; she had seen enough to know that civilization strikes no deeper in human nature than clothes go to change the man.

"Civilized?" Don Jose had taken her up. "Ah, madam, already wild tales reach us of the Germans in Belgium."

"But there was a treaty," she cried, "and the greatest nations in the world have guaranteed the neutrality of Belgium. Germany herself—"

"True!" said Jose; "but it is because of the violation of Belgian neutrality, among other things, that England has entered the war, it is said."

"Ah-h!" said Harrigan, lapsing suddenly from Spanish into his Irish brogue. "Thrue for ye, man! John Bull will take the Kaiser by the throat. In time of peace, why, to hell with England, say I, like all good Irishmen; but in time av war-r, it's shoulder to shoulder, John Bull an' Paddy, say I, an' we'll lick the wor-r-rld!"

And McTee broke in savagely. "You forget the Scotch. Without the Scotch, England and Ireland—what could they do? Nothing!"

"Could they not?" said Harrigan, with rising temper. "I tell ye, ye black Highlander, that wan Irishman—"

"Hush," said Kate earnestly; for the Spaniard was staring at them in amaze. "It is a world war, and no time for jealousy. England—Scotland —Ireland—and America, too, in time—we will all be fighting for one purpose. And when the last test comes, the United States—"

She stopped with a gesture of pride, and Harrigan said with deep feeling: "Aye, they're a hard lot, the Yankees. But as for the Scotch," he went on in a murmur which only McTee could hear—"as for the Scotch, I wouldn't be wipin' my feet on 'em, when it comes to the fightin'. D'ye hear me, McTee?"

"And understand," said McTee, smiling broadly, so that none of the rest might understand; "our time is close at hand, Harrigan. We're on dry land."

"We are—thank God," answered Harrigan, "but play the game, McTee, till the girl is cared for."

In the meantime Senor Jose had explained to Kate the nearness of the city—El Ciudad Grande—for she had been asking many urgent questions. The upshot of their conversation was that their host offered to take them immediately into the town, where they could find accommodation at the one hotel—if they refused his further hospitality. So in half an hour Senor Jose's carriage of state was harnessed and the four journeyed into El Ciudad Grande.

Senor Jose went with them to explain to the hotel owner that these were his guests—his dear friends—his friends of many years' standing—in fact, his relatives in close blood. In short, he recommended the party to the special care of the hotelkeeper. Business called the hospitable Spaniard away. He refused to accept any consideration for the clothes which he donated to the party, and McTee jingled a handful of Henshaw's gold in vain. Senor Jose must depart, but he would return the next day. So the three stood alone together at last. Harrigan was the first to speak.

"I've an engagement. I'm afther havin' some important business on hand, Kate, colleen, so I'll be steppin' out." And he turned to go.

"Wait," she called. "I know what your engagements are when the Irish comes so thick on your tongue, Dan. You were about to have an engagement also, Angus?"

McTee glowered on Harrigan for having so clumsily betrayed them.

"You are like children," she said softly, "and you let me read your minds."

She bowed her head in long thought.

Then: "Didn't we pass the sign of the British consul down the street over that little building?"

"Yes," said McTee, wondering, and again she was lost in thought.

Then she raised her head and stepped close to them with that smile, half whimsical and half sad.

"I'm going to ask you to let me be alone for a time—for a long time. It will be sunset in five hours. Will you let me have that long to do some hard thinking? And will you promise me during that time that you will not fly at each other's throats the moment you are out of my sight? For what I will have to say at sunset I know will make a great deal of difference in your attitude to each other."

"I'll promise," said Harrigan suddenly. "I've waited so long—I can stand five hours more."

"I'll promise," said McTee; but he scowled upon the floor.

CHAPTER 39

THEY LEFT her and walked from the hotel. At the door Harrigan turned fiercely upon the Scotchman.

"Do what ye please for the five hours, McTee, but give me the room I need for breathin'. D'ye hear? Otherwise I'll be forgettin' me promises."

"Do I hear ye?" answered McTee, snarling. "Aye, growl while you may. I'll stop that throat of yours for good—tonight."

He turned on his heel, and the two men separated. Harrigan struck with a long swing out over a road which led into the rolling fields near the little town. He walked rapidly, and his thoughts kept pace, for he was counting his chances to win Kate as a miser counts his hoard of gold. Two pictures weighed large in his mind. One was of Kate at ease in the home of the Spaniard. Such ease would never be his; she came from another social world—a higher sphere. The second picture was of McTee climbing down from the wireless house and calmly assuming command of the mutineers in the crisis. Such a maneuver would never have occurred to the Irishman, and it was only through that maneuver that the ship had been brought to shore, for nothing save the iron will of McTee could have directed the mutineers.

When the sun hung low, he turned and strode back toward the village, and despair trailed him like his shadow.

He began to see clearly now what he had always feared. She loved McTee—McTee, who spoke clear, pure English, when he chose, and who could talk of many things. She loved McTee, but she dared not avow that love for fear of infuriating Harrigan and thereby risking the life of the Scotchman. It grew plainer and plainer. With the thought of Kate came another, far different, and yet blending one with another. When he reached the village, it was still a short time before sunset. He went straight to the British consulate and entered, for he had reached the solution of his puzzle.

"My name's Harrigan," he said to the little man with the sideburns and the studious eyes, "and I've come to know if the old country has sent for volunteers. I want to go over."

"The old country," said the consul, "has called for volunteers, and I have discovered a means of sending our boys across the water; but"—and here he examined Harrigan shrewdly—"but it's an easy thing to take an Irish name. How am I to know you're not a German, my friend? I've never seen you before."

Harrigan swelled.

"A German? Me?" he muttered, and then, his head tilted back: "Ye little wan-eyed, lantern-jawed, flat-headed block, is it me—is it Harrigan ye call a German? Shtep out from behind the desk an' let me see av you're a man!"

Strangely enough, the consul did not seem irritated by this outburst. He was, in fact, smiling. Then his hand went out to the Irishman.

"Mr. Harrigan," he said, "I'm honored by knowing you."

Harrigan stared and accepted the hand with caution; there was still battle in his eyes.

"And can you send me over?" he asked doubtfully.

"I can. As I said before, we've raised a small fund for just this purpose."

He drew out a piece of paper and commenced taking down the particulars of Harrigan's name and birth and other details. Then a short typewritten note signed by the consul ended the interview. He gave Harrigan directions about how he could reach a shipping agent on the eastern coast, handed over the note, and the Irishman stepped out of the little office already on his way to the world war. He took no pleasure in his resolution, but wandered slowly back toward the hotel with downward head. He would speak a curt farewell and step out of the lives of the two. It would be very simple unless McTee showed some exultation, but if he did—Here Harrigan refused to think further.

It was well after sunset when he crossed the veranda, and at the door he found McTee striding up and down.

"Harrigan," said McTee.

"Well?", growled Harrigan.

"Stand over here close to me, and keep your face shut while I'm speaking. It won't take me long."

The words were insulting enough, but the voice which spoke them was sadly subdued.

"Listen," said McTee. "What I've got to say is harder for me to do than anything I've ever done in my life. So don't make me repeat anything. Harrigan, I've tried to beat you by fair means or foul ever since we met—ever since you saved my hide in the Ivilei district of Honolulu. I've tried to get you down, and I've failed. I fought you"—here he ground his teeth in agony—"and you beat me."

"It was the bucking of the deck that beat you," put in Harrigan.

"Shut up till I'm through or I'll wring your neck and break your back! I've failed to down you, Harrigan. You beat me on the Mary Rogers. You made a fool of me on the island. And on the Heron—"

He paused again, breathing hard.

"On the *Heron* , it was you who brought us food and water when we were dying. And afterward, when Henshaw died, I jumped out before the mutineers and took command of them because I thought I could win back in Kate's mind any ground which I'd lost before. I paraded the deck before her eyes; I gave commands; I was the man of the hour; I was driving the *Heron* to the shore in spite of the fire."

"You were," admitted Harrigan sadly. "It was a great work you did, McTee. It was that which won her—"

"But even when I was in command, you proved yourself the better man, Harrigan."

The Irishman leaned back against the wall, gasping, weak with astonishment.

McTee went on: "I paraded the deck; I made a play to make her admire me, and for a while I succeeded, until the time came when you were carried up to the deck too weak to keep the men at work in the fireroom. Ah, Harrigan, that was a great moment to me. I said to Kate: 'Harrigan has done well, but of course he can't control men—his mind is too simple.'"

"Did you say that?" murmured Harrigan, and hatred made his voice soft, almost reverent.

"I did, and I went on: 'I suppose I'll have to go down there and drive the lads back to their work.' So down I went, but you know what happened. They wouldn't work for me. They stood around looking stupid at me and left me alone in the fireroom, and I had to come back on deck, in the sight of Kate, and rouse you out of your sleep and beg you to go back and try to make the lads keep at their work. And you got up to your knees, struggling to get back your consciousness! And you staggered to your feet, and you called to the firemen who lay senseless and sick on the deck around you—sick for sleep—and when they heard you call, they got up, groaning, and they reeled after you back to their work in the fireroom, and some of them dragged themselves along on their hands and knees. Oh, God!"

He struck his clenched fist across his eyes.

"And all the time I was watching the awe and the wonder come up like a fire in the eyes of Kate, while she looked after you."

Harrigan watched him with the same stupid amazement.

"Harrigan," said McTee at last, "you've won her. When I walked out by myself today, I saw that I was the only obstacle between her and her happiness. She doesn't dare tell you she loves you, for fear that I'll try to kill you. So I've decided to step out from between—I *have* stepped out! I'm going back to Scotland and get into the war. If I have fighting enough, I can forget the girl, maybe, and you! I've talked to the British consul already, and he's given me a note that will take me over the water. So, Harrigan, I've merely come to say good-by to you— and you can say good-by for me to Kate."

"Wait," said Harrigan. "There are a good many kinds of fools, but a Scotch fool is the worst of all. Take that paper out of your pocket and tear it up. Ah-h, McTee, ye blind man! Can't ye see that gir-rl's been eatin' out her hear-rt for the love av ye, damn your eyes? Can't ye see that the only thing that keeps her from throwin' her ar-rms around your neck is the fear of Harrigan? Look!"

He pulled out the note which the consul had given him.

"I've got the same thing you have. I'm going to go over the water. I tell you, I've seen her eyes whin she looked at ye, McTee, an' that's how I know she loves ye. Tear up your paper! A blight on ye! May ye have long life and make the girl happy—an' rot in hell after!"

"By God," said McTee, "we've both been thinking the same thing at the same time. And maybe we're both wrong. Kate said she had something to say to us. Let's see her first and hear her speak."

"It'll break my heart to hear her confess she loves ye, McTee—but I'll go!"

They went to the sleepy clerk behind the desk and asked him to send up word to Miss Malone that they wished to see her.

"Ah, Miss Malone," said the clerk, nodding, "before she left—"

"Left?" echoed the two giants in voices of thunder.

"She gave me this note to deliver to you."

And he passed them the envelope. Each of them placed a hand upon it and stared stupidly at the other.

"Open it!" said Harrigan hoarsely.

"I'm troubled with my old failing—a weakness of the eyes," said McTee. "Open it yourself."

Harrigan opened it at last and drew out the paper within. They stood under a light, shoulder to shoulder, and read with difficulty, for the hand of Harrigan which held the paper shook.

Dear lads, dear Dan and Angus:

As soon as you left me, I went to the British consul, and from him I learned the shortest way of cutting across country to the railroad. By the time you read this, I am on the train and speeding north to the States.

I have known for a long time that the only thing which keeps you from being fast friends is the love which each of you says he has for me. So I have decided to step from between you, for there is nothing on earth so glorious as the deep friendship of one strong man for another.

I fear you may try to follow me, but I warn you that it would be useless. I have taken a course of training, and I am qualified as a nurse. The Red Cross of America will soon be sending units across the water to care for the wounded of the Allies. I shall go with one of the first units. You might be able to trace me to the States, but you will never be able to trace me overseas. This is good-by.

It is hard to say it in writing. I want to take your hands and tell you how much you mean to me. But I could not wait to do that. For your own sakes I have to flee from you both.

Now that I have said good-by, it is easier to add another thing. I care for both of you more than for any man I have ever known, but one of you I love with all my soul. Even now I dare not say which, for it might make enmity and jealousy between you, and enmity between such men as you means only one thing—death.

I have tried to find courage to stand before you and say which of you I love, but I cannot. At the last moment I grow weak at the thought of the battle which would follow. My only resort is to resign him I care for beyond all friends, and him I love beyond all other men.

I know that when I am gone, you will become fast friends, and together you will be kings of men. And in time—for a man's life is filled with actions which rub out all memories—you will forget that you loved me, I know; but perhaps you will not forget that because I resigned you both, I built a foundation of rock for your friendship.

You will be happy, you will be strong, you will be true to one another. And for that I am glad. But to you whom I love: Oh, my dear, it is breaking my heart to leave you!

Kate

One hand of each was on the paper as they lowered it and stared into each other's face, with a black doubt, and a wild hope. Then of one accord they raised the paper and read it through again.

"And to think," muttered Harrigan at last, "that I should have ruined her happiness. I could tear my heart out, McTee!"

"Harrigan," said the big Scotchman solemnly, "it is you she means. See! She cried over the paper while she was writing. No woman could weep for Black McTee!"

"And no woman could write like that to Harrigan. Angus, you can keep the knowledge that she loves you, but let me keep the letter. Ah-h, McTee, I'll be afther keepin' it forninst me heart!"

"Let's go outside," said McTee. "There is no air in this room."

They went out into the black night, and as they walked, each kept his hand upon the letter, so that it seemed to be a power which tied them together.

"Angus," said Harrigan after a time, "we'll be fightin' for the letter soon. Why should we? I know every line of it by heart."

"I know every word," answered McTee.

"I've a thought," said Harrigan. "In the ould days, whin a great man died, they used to burn his body. An' now I'm feelin' as if somethin' had died in me— the hope av winnin' Kate, McTee. So let's burn her letter between us, eh?"

"Harrigan," said McTee with heartfelt emotion, "that thought is well worthy of you!"

They knelt on the little spot. They placed the paper between them. Each scratched a match and lighted one side of the paper; the flames rose and met in the middle of the letter. Yet they did not watch the progress of the fire; by the sudden flare of light they gazed steadily into each other's face, straining their eyes as the light died away as though each had discovered in the other something new and strange. When they looked down, the paper was merely a dim, red glow which passed away as quickly as a flush dies from the face, and the wind carried away the frail ashes. Then they rose and walked shoulder to shoulder on and into the night.